"Needled"

Book One
In the Dr. Ma Mystery Series

By Lenore Maio

Dedication

To my family, friends, patients, and clients, who inspire me every day.

To my long suffering spouse, for the time I take in my projects, I dedicate this book to you. You are such a great friend. If this book breaks into the hearts and minds of readers, we will celebrate.

To my Tech support guy, Barron Snyder, one of the finest men I have known. Thank you.

To my friend, Melissa Geil. Thank you for the education and assistance.

To anyone out there, starting to write their first piece of fiction. Having the courage and vision to 'see' is simple. Taking the time to 'say' is more complex. Translating your story, to a Universal language, is well, a work in progress.

Thank you.

Introduction....from the Author

We are different you and I. Oh, not in the usual sense, where we are all unique. No. Rather, we differ in a more profound sense.

A yawning chasm often exists, between a speaker and a listener. This chasm may only be crossed by a bridge, created from experiences. There is little hope of this crossing for so many.

As the author of this book, I have experienced what is written here, but what of the listener? The reader? So many wrap their lives in the petty what ifs and why nots. You cannot experience anything real, while wrapped in that protective cocoon.

How do you explain the smell of real blood at a murder scene, when the reader has not been there? So few, thankfully, can say that the mingling of blood, sweat soured by fear, and the expression of bodily wastes in a traumatic death, provide a familiar fragrance.

I will provide a bridge of words for you to cross, dear reader, if you so desire. Perhaps we will meet in the middle, with a greater understanding of each other. Perhaps we will find complete familiarity.

There is little in this book that is fantasy. Truth is often very strange. Good luck within these pages, finding your way across.

Prologue

When an event, such as sudden death, traumatic injury, or great suffering, happens in this world, tiny tears in the fabric of the Universe occur.

Nothing heals these defects in that fabric. They remain scars, evidence of the event, for all time.

When the rip of the Universal fabric occurs, certain ears are tuned to the sound. They are here for that very purpose. To listen.

Sentinels, Guardians, Elementals, Spirits, and a host of otherworldly manifestations, watch us live our lives. Some may help, some may watch, some may take advantage, and some may manipulate, for evil purposes.

This is the story of one Elemental being, who sticks around year after year, to do all she can, for you, and for me.

Table of Contents

Chapter One - Just A Morning Run

Daylight was just breaking when Dr. Ma left the house. Her morning run was the first event of the day. She wouldn't start without it.

Dr. Ma, often referred to simply as 'Ma,' was a creature of habit. Her Chinese surname was Ma, which meant horse. But she was not Chinese. The name had been given to her, by the Chinese born doctors in graduate school.

The habit of an early morning run, allowed her to organize her mind. A somewhat tangled mind, fully aware, even after millennia of existence. Yes, she was old, very old.

Dr. Ma turned her face skywards, as the infant sun wriggled out of its protective evening cocoon. She loved the way it painted the sky, a wash of silvers and grays.

Body on auto pilot, she tapped out a steady rhythm with her feet. One, two, three footfalls, and one breath. Repeat. Physical exertion gave her new perspective on any issues left from the previous day. The last 24 hours that is. Day and night were one cycle for her anymore.

She didn't sleep. She hadn't for centuries. She could go as deep as delta, her brain waves working .5 cycles per second. She could not go deeper, yet. If there was a deeper. She believed so. In delta, a deep meditative state, with her eyes closed, and her body deathly still, she received the recharge she needed for her human body.

Her brain was moving along as quickly as her feet. Life in general, her patient's cases or the week's plans would be stirred gently like puzzle pieces waiting to be selected for a board. What fit, would gently be placed in its proper location. She liked seeing the whole picture.

Dr. Ma was a Traditional Chinese Medical Doctor. Optimal health maintenance and disease prevention was the center of her life's philosophy. She maintained her body with diet and exercise. Lean muscle rippled under wrinkle free skin even at fifty five human years old.

A mass of inky black hair, was pulled tightly into a long braid down her back while running or working out. Impossibly straight, it reached to her waist when unbound.

The South Florida humidity and warmth, were good for her lungs. In Florida, the humidity was always present. More in the summer, and less in the Winter. Winter was just three months long here, at best.

Mile one. Time to pick up the pace.

One of her patients, a retired world class water skier, had just stopped smoking. He should never have started. She told him to start walking early in the morning, by the ocean, to help restore his lung tissue. She hoped he followed her advice. Patients tend to disregard advice.

Muscle contractions pushed early morning sluggishness and toxins out of her pores. Sweat! More efficient than urine to get rid of toxins, hands down.

Typical of any cardio based athlete, Dr. Ma's heart was larger, from years of stressing it, to move blood to each fingertip and toe and back again. Athlete's Heart is what its called. Her resting heart rate was about 45 beats per minute.

Terry, one of her patients, recently told her that his insurance premiums had gone up. His new doctor misdiagnosed this condition thinking his slow heart rate was bad. Terry was a 65 year old world class athlete and an amazing physical specimen. Dr. Ma had suggested a change in doctors.

"Preferably, to one with half a brain," she had muttered to herself after leaving the exam room.

Dr. Ma saw Terry and Marla, his fit and healthy wife, out running almost daily. In Ma's opinion, the insurance company should reward Terry and Marla by decreasing what they paid. Dr. Ma was sure to never get a job selling insurance if alternative medicine didn't work out.

Mile two. She increased her pace another notch.

Making the turn as usual on Summa Street, she headed towards Flagler Drive. Running easily, she was enjoying the early morning as bright sunlight broke over Palm Beach Island. She headed north

Scents of the surrounding foliage were mixed, but muted, as she ran. The sun hadn't warmed the leaves and flowers yet. More heat would lift dew off the plant leaves, mixing unique scent combinations into the air to enjoy.

As Dr. Ma got closer to the Intracoastal Waterway, the scent mixture was increasingly tinged with a salty overlay. She was roughly half a mile from the ocean sands of Palm Beach Island.

Salty sea air, mixed with humidity, was even better for the lungs. The salty tang was strongest when running the beach. You had the entertainment of Sandpipers, crabs and, this time of year, the man-o-war. In Palm Beach the Sandboni made any early morning workout more of a challenge with the long trenches it left in the sand.

Taking in the full scope of beautiful homes on her left, and the expanse of Intracoastal Waterway on her right, she gave thanks to the Universal design that blessed her chosen path for this lifetime.

"How many lifetimes has it been?" she mused "Too many lives to remember and no reason to care how many more." Each time was just her job and she did it well.

Jumping up on the short wall next to the sidewalk, she quickly passed as the shallow water lapped at the rocks, sand, and scrub trees, forming the wall's base.

Little crabs ducked into their sand holes, firmly convinced that she presented some vague threat. Too bad humans had lost such a refined instinct for survival. The crabs will still be here and the humans will become extinct at this rate. Dr. Ma figured that humans may just kill themselves off with crazy lifestyles, before violence and genetic mutation could do it for them. I will be out of a job when that happens. No humans, no need for my help anymore.

Even worse, the dietary choices and abuses people piled on themselves amazed her. Binges, followed by fad diets, addictions to drugs, alcohol and sugar laden foods, were producing a population of sicker, fatter and sadder people.

She appreciated the early morning exercisers and their pets getting out to give themselves a healthy boost. She made sure to smile and wave at everyone she saw.

Dr. Ma was a vegetarian, consuming eggs but no cheese, or milk. She had an interest in eggs that came from her ancient origins, but tried to eat them no more than a few times a week. She paid through the nose for those pasture raised, hormone and antibiotic free, organic, non GMO, etc., etc., etc., eggs. There was barely room on the box top for all the things the eggs *weren't.*

She was coming up on the big tree as the path curved past Desota Road. The tree was a time-less presence. "How many years have you stood there, old man?" she thought.
Ma knew the tree spirit personally. Jamil was his name. He was the current guardian of a powerful ley line that ran through the State of Florida. They had worked together many times in the past. She was glad to see him again. He had saved her life once.

"Ma Sama," Jamil the tree nodded impercepti-bly.

"Great One," Ma nodded back, slowing her pace slightly.

She reached out her hand for a brief touch of the hard scrabbled bark. So many layers of time had shaped that brown and crumpled skin.

Mentally, she thanked the long serving guardian. Ma wondered how many passed him every day, and recognized him for what he real-ly was. As the world aged, these guardians were slowly dying off. She frowned at the impli-cation of a world without them.

Trees his age were rare. Dr. Ma thought they brought grace to the landscape with their gnarled branches and massive trunks.

Guardians were no longer well known to humanity. So many mystical beings had faded from human thought through the millennia.

Today, it seemed to her, there was the lowest levels of belief and recognition for otherworldly creatures. There certainly was a plethora of books and movies describing them. They even used them as main characters. Everyone thought of it as merely entertainment.

Did the fantasy genre aficionados really expect a water Sprite to be floating on their back in the Intracoastal waterway? Right here off of Flagler Drive?

The actual Sprites, he or she, Ma could never tell the difference, were at this moment, watching the walkers and runners out for their daily exercise. She could see them, and others like them, as easily as any other thing visible on the various planes of existence.

Quite a variety of otherworldly creatures could be gathered around Jamil any day she passed by him. Such entities were a magnet or maybe more like a vortex, pulling things to their center from the co-existing planes.

There were seven by the way. Seven planes of existence that could be seen. Planes that could house various forms of life.

She herself was an otherworldly creature. Dr. Ma was an Elemental who chose service on Earth not once, but many times. She was a perfect example of matter simply changing form. This little fact was undiscovered by humans yet, and staying that way, she hoped.

The laws of atomic physics, explain that matter only changes form. Bits and pieces rearranged themselves constantly. There was no major coming and going, as the Judeo-Christian ethic would have you believe. Entities such as Dr. Ma just rearranged more pieces at a time, seamlessly.

"Focus!" she reprimanded herself. She almost ran over a small dog darting between the other exercisers along the path. The dog stopped short and stared at her. Then, it growled and tucked tail, before running back to its owner.

Her smooth tanned skin, tightly muscled body, and startling lapis blue eyes seemed a flawless mask of her true Elemental self. The blue eyes were not a choice. David, the other doctor in her practice, and another Elemental, had them too. They all did. It was a definite 'tell' if you knew what you were looking for.

Animals and some children could see her true nature, but it was the rare adult who did. Most often they just felt something was off. She knew a homeless person or two who could see her clearly. Mistakenly, these folks were thought to be mentally ill.

In days gone by, creatures like her were accepted. Acceptance and inclusion, well, that would require belief in mystical creatures to be absolute, and even mainstream. "Never going to happen," she thought, shaking her head at the impossibility of such a notion.

Dr. Ma didn't bother to make many close friends. You can't go around giving folks the jitters for some reason they can't explain, and then expecting them to come over for dinner.

She also had a job to do. That was why she was here after all, wasn't it? She and David, her constant companion, made the return journey lifetime after lifetime. The perks of the return visit were obvious! The heady smell of roses, cut grass and baking muffins were just a few examples.

"Muffins!" she thought. Dr. Ma's stomach gave a slight murmur in remembrance. She had baked an aromatic batch of gluten free, banana flax, hemp, and chia seed muffins this morning. The ripe banana, vanilla extract, cinnamon spice, and toasted macadamia nuts that coated the firm, crisp skinned tops was intoxicating. They were a treat for her assistant Winnie's, birthday today.

There was one cooling on the counter right now, calling her name. She could manage to have hers' before Winnie and David without criticism. A lifetime of high level physical activity had left her with almost unnoticeable body fat, regardless of how many muffins she ate.

David, her companion for the last thousand years, had a physique more stunning then hers. Yet, unless Winnie stopped him, he was likely to consume as many of the muffins on the plate as possible today.

They had been together for a millennia, her and David, but never romantic, never sexual. They were as intimate as they could be with their endless lives. Made closer by the soul changing events they had fought through, side by side.

Ma's own soulmate, had passed beyond the planes of existence she currently frequented. Passed, so long ago. Dragons mate for life, and Ma was a dragon. Her stomach rumbled again, interrupting memories she preferred to keep buried.

"Yes," she thought. "A muffin when she got home sounded perfect. Maybe a second later today." The dozen she had baked would cover the three of them. Maybe Bud, Winnie's husband, would get one as well. If any muffins made it home with Winnie.

Bud was a big fan of Dr. Ma's baking. Well, actually he was a big fan of all her cooking. She smiled, thinking of their last dinner together. For someone who loved to cook, an appreciative eater was the best compliment.

Mile three! Up to four strides per breath now.

Increasing her speed, she kept with her plan of negative splits for her six to seven mile route. That meant running each mile faster than the last one.

Every time the wall she was running on ended at another dock walkway, she jumped. She would land on both feet and drive one leg up to the other side. She alternated driving legs each time.

Those legs would be burning on the run back, but she had to throw in a bit of cross training when the opportunity presented itself. It had been a busy season with patients at the clinic.

Dr. Ma used to run off road. Unfortunately, that took time driving there that she didn't seem to have lately. She loved the feeling of anonymity among the trees and scrub that the local mountain bike trails provided. Adrenaline from avoiding being run over by a speeding mountain biker, didn't hurt either.

She passed the Church before Edmore Rd. Next came St. Catherine's Greek Orthodox Church. They were both on her left. Finally she took the eastbound turn onto the Southern Boulevard causeway and Bingham Island.

Bingham Island and it's Audubon Preserve were the source of the winged predators birds, mainly Osprey, that devastated the local small bird population each year.

Audubon held a long term lease for the island from the Bingham family. It was an ideal nesting and hunting location. Dr. Ma liked birds. All birds, actually.

Being a dragon, she was able to talk to birds. Her favorite? The Crow. Crows were the acknowledged messenger of deceased spirits to the living. Birds, were a source of information for Dr. Ma.

She ran over the Intracoastal Waterway. There was a fabulous view south towards the Lake Worth Lagoon and north to Palmsicle Island, that little dab of dirt and trees in the middle of the waterway.

On the north side of the causeway, you could park and walk along the sandy beach or swim. A narrow stretch of thin grass allowed for picnics to be set up or kids to run and play. There was parking on the south side in order to fish off the Southern Boulevard bridge. Thick metal fencing kept humans out of the Preserve proper.

Looking south and running easily, a scent came to her. Like getting a whiff of someone's backyard barbecue you can't determine the origin of, she felt the Wind coming. No ordinary wind, it

was a psychic storm. Dense and palpable energy gathered together and headed her way.

Someone had died. Recently. Tragically.
Someone specifically coming to her, to tell her
everything, to involve her in the gruesome details, to make her take their baggage as they
passed unburdened from this life.

She would be the keeper of their death memory, until the perpetrator was caught. This is what
she did, what she signed up for. A spiritual go
between in heinous criminal matters. Matters
usually involving otherworldly beings. Killing
someone that is.

Dr. Ma thought back to what, a couple thousand
years ago, wasn't it? Time becomes a blur
when you are enjoying yourself right? As a
ranking member of Solomon's magical guard,
(magicians and other worldly entities working
paid or not for King Solomon) you could absorb
the details from such a Wind, and simply go kill
the perpetrator.

This was the easiest way to restore Universal
balance from such an act.

She focused her inner eye while keeping her
outside ones open, to better see the coming

Spirit storm. Getting caught by an appearance of any Wind was less than desirable during a run but overall it couldn't be helped.

She would do the best she could, under the circumstances. After all, this had happened before. There was no altering the cosmos. It chose its own path.
If you were in the way, well, you had better move, or adapt, because it wasn't changing course for any puny human. In her case, she wasn't exactly puny, or even really human, but you get the idea.

It looked like she was going to be involved in another murder investigation. That seemed to be what she did, aside from treating patients, and teaching martial arts classes. Or, supporting various charities. Dr. Ma enjoyed sharing what she had amassed through the millennia, by giving to charity. Savings plans that go on for a thousand years or so, can really add up.

"Damn! She had a charity event tonight she was committed to!" she thought. She almost forgot for a moment with the Wind approaching. Hopefully, the circumstances would not interfere with her attendance later.

The last murder case that she and David helped investigate, was complicated by funds stolen from a charity. They had caught the perps and written a nice check to replace the funds anonymously.

The scent or 'smell' of the Wind was getting stronger now. This was when you would know if it was chicken or beef on the barbecue grill, but little else.

Unfortunately, the appearance of the Wind, was not going to promise the entertainment and enjoyment of the barbecue image. Just the intense feeling of its arrival was enough to know things were going to be happening, and soon.

Not even mile four yet and it was most definitely *show time*.

Her tanned skin broke out in a rash of goosebumps. Her vision changed, ever so slightly. Objects around her seemed farther away, as if they had to make room for the crowding in of the other dimension.

She hoped nobody was noticing a woman running a bit unsteadily, now, as she came off the east end of the bridge. She lifted her head and gave the coming storm a grim smile.

"Hello Wind," she said to herself. "Bring it on."

Chapter Two - The Wind

Starting to walk along the roadway, east of the bridge, she found her way to one of the trees lining the causeway and leaned against it. In moments, the familiar chills of the Wind's arrival ran through her body.

"David, are you there?" She reached out with her mind towards her companion. The one she needed to help her weather the psychic event. When David held things steady for her, she could extract the maximum amount of information from the storm of emotions. The Wind was the departed Spirit's jumble of thoughts and feelings at the time of death.

Dr. Ma could smell the coming Wind. It was not truly a definable scent, like chocolate, or flowers. There would be a howling noise the Wind made without the event making a sound to human ears.

Like a far away warning, with no identifiable characteristics, there was just a sense of something approaching that would materialize like a freight train, bearing down as it got closer and closer. She would try to be smack in the middle of the tracks.

"Hey, David, hello?" She reached out again. "Today? Any time now!"

She had no love of this 'gift,' as some misguided folks like to call it, when a human, or not quite a human, could see and hear Spirits. There was no sense of timing, or propriety, when Spirits decided to involve anyone in their issues. In her case, it was merely her job.

She signed up for it every time it was offered. Well, that was another story, for another time. At least she wasn't driving today when the Wind decided to make its entrance. You have to pull over to a safe spot to park and wait it through, if you were driving.

The images of the causeway around and in front of her blurred even more It was, as if, something passed in front of them. It was similar to how you could see through the shimmer of heat, rising from pavement in summer. The clarity of what you saw was changed, but not gone.

Thanks! Finally! There was that strange and welcome opening, like a door or window in the fabric of her mind. Dr. Ma watched as David paused in the middle of his Tai Chi routine. This was happening before his morning class began, so he was alone in the dojo.

He had heard her calling. David was looking directly at her through the veil of time and space that currently separated them. He gave her one of his 100 watt smiles. "Morning!" he mouthed silently. Then he grinned.

David was a true warrior spirit. Like Dr. Ma, he loved a challenge. There are always some strange folks out there that relish a challenge. Those that grin like a banshee when the shit hits the proverbial fan. They run toward the chaos with abandon, and are happy that it would momentarily invade the routine of daily life. That was her David.

"About time you tuned in!" Dr. Ma said softly, relieved to see him. She looked around to make sure nobody was noticing her talking to herself, while holding up a tree. So far, so good. Humans were in general self absorbed. They noticed little outside of their own small orbit.

She returned his slightly maniacal grin and nodded. *Show time.* She needed him to anchor her. Quickly. Anchoring wasn't complicated, for someone with David's strength and ability. Done right, and it would make a major difference. Well, depending on the strength of the coming Spirit Wind.

She watched David assess the situation as she stood there. She shivered slightly with anticipation and said, "Hurry." She urged him on, even as she tucked her arm around the slender tree.

Florida Scrub, or Sand pines, were a little scratchy to hug. The tree's bark seemed to match his personality, as she felt him nudge her energetically. It was a clear, "well move off then," in tree speak. He didn't want her using him as a prop for the Wind event. Trees were very sentient, and this particular tree was less than overjoyed at her choice of location.

"Not just yet," she murmured. "You'll be fine." The flowing pulse of the tree's life energy paused and restarted. The tree version of a derisive snort, she assumed.

The coming psychic event, now appeared like a complete tear in the fabric of the air around her. Forget the soft blurring of images, this was a full on rip. Oddly, it showed her location, on its perimeter, David, in the empty dojo across from her, and something else between them, blossoming.

Slowly unravelling in that space in the center, she knew from experience, would be the scene of the crime. The scene of a gruesome crime. A murder.

Dr. Ma and David had done this many times before. They were old pro's. The idea was to anchor and stabilize your mind, staying in the middle of the storm, as long as possible. She wanted every bit of information she could absorb. As much as she could handle, about the crime.

The space between them grew, squeezing them and distorting their images. Around them, the scene unfolded. David cocked his head. He too could hear the Spirit Wind, howling audibly, as it arrived.

Dr. Ma could still see her surroundings. A bit hazy, but she was sure nobody lounging swimming or playing along the causeway saw or heard the Wind, or they would have been screaming and running for cover.

David mouthed "Are you ready?" It was impossible to really hear him in this altered reality, but the meaning was clear. In a pinch she could read lips.

She nodded in agreement. David closed his eyes to concentrate and she followed suit. What she was looking at was inside her anyway. The events played out like a movie reel in her mind. Sometimes so tangible it seemed they were a part of her very being. Smells, sounds, sensations, all integrated into her own, until it was hard to tell them apart for a time.

All was ready.

Dr. Ma often thought how odd it would appear to normal humans if the storm was whipping around her in real time. Her hair would be blown into a massive black cloud, her body swaying, her face set in grim determination, concentrating on the images being shown to her.

Yep, that would have been a trip to the looney bin for all reporting on that one.

David began his Tai Chi practice again. He wasn't at all distracted. Far from it. He was using the practice to collect energy, spinning the ball of Qi between his hands to a North and South position, and forming a safety net.

Her safety net.

He began to compress the energy, slowing the pace of the Wind. Dr. Ma expelled the breath she forgot she was holding and relaxed into the sounds, sights and smells associated with a traumatic demise.

This was a S*pirit's* Wind that approached and enveloped her. When a human Spirit experienced significant trauma, especially in death, it leaves tiny tears in the fabric of the Universe. Through those rents in the fabric passes the Wind of that spirit.

Dr. Ma always thought that the Spirit passed wherever they wish to go. As a follower of the Tao, she believed in the power that surrounds and flows through all things. Tao meant the way, or the path you followed spiritually.

She knew that a human being simply changes form when they die. They don't wink out of existence. Sadly, for the loved ones and friends surviving after that death, the continued existence of the Spirit is not sufficient. Humans want to touch, hold and talk to their family and friends. Unless you were gifted to communicate across the veil between the dimensions, this wasn't going to happen.

Dr. Ma taught meditation, Qigong and Tai Chi, and other martial arts classes with David at their dojo. With training and focus most human beings have some ability to sense or even interact with spiritual energy. Fewer however can feel, touch or interact with the spirit after death.

Dr. Ma would teach students that the Tao, regulates natural processes like birth and death. It establishes and restores balance in the Universe. Like its famous representation of Yin and Yang, commonly shown in black and white, it embodies the harmony of opposites.

Look carefully at the Yin Yang symbol, so well known around the world, and you will see several important things. One is that each color has a body and a tail. It may look like a clearly defined shape. Not correct. It better represents one color flowing into the other, where each tail wraps the body of the opposite color.

If the image is rendered correctly, there will be a tiny dot of the opposite color within the large body of the black and the white. This is there to clarify that neither color, Yin or Yang is ever really in existence without a bit of the other contained within.

So, when we change our form in death we still retain that tiny bit of life connection in our center. Just as surely, we had that tiny part of our impending death within us while we were still here.

Dr. Ma opened herself fully to absorb the entire event brought to her by the departing spirit. This must have been a significant trauma for it to have so much psychic energy available. The Wind it brought was very strong.

"Did the crime occur rather close to her current location? Is that why?" Ma thought.

David was using his considerable strength, physical and mental, to hold the events images almost still. The Spirit Wind swallowed Dr. Ma, hovering while it delivered its 'message.'

Finally arriving in full, the sounds of screaming pierced through her. The smells, tastes, and as she opened her inner vision, the sights of what had happened, saturated her. Every pore absorbed as much information as possible and when she could not hold any more she nodded to David, closing her inner eyes.

She was ready to be done with this intrusion. No matter how much you want to help, no matter how well you do your job, we all have our limitations.

David spun the ball of Qi from North and South, to East and West, then open. The wind coalesced into its original path of movement through her and passed beyond.

The temporary window between David and Dr. Ma closed, fading away.

The Spirit moved off to its unknown destination. Ma felt the Spirit's sadness lift, as the trauma in Ma's dimension no longer imprisoned the recent murder victim in all her pain and suffering. The images around her stilled, and coalesced into the day as it was before the Wind's arrival. She found she had released her near death grip on the reluctant tree.

Dr. Ma took several deep breaths and starting walking east. She was running again by the time she reached the little bridge on SR98 where it officially joined Southern Boulevard with Palm Beach Island proper.

Ma was like a magnet for the Wind. That was her job wasn't it? You just couldn't beat the benefits package in this line of work. Kidding, what benefits exactly? Obligation to help a departed Spirit after their traumatic death?

These Winds, were more often than not, created by a Spirit recently passing. They didn't want to leave quietly, no, they had something significant to say.

The Spirit could have died suddenly and traumatically. The Spirit could have been really angry that they died, but not suffered a bit on the way out. Other random possibilities could be in play.

The Spirit could also have been a powerful Adept, magician, psychic, otherworldly and so forth. Those type usually had enough power to stir a strong Wind if they needed to leave a message behind.

It seemed they always had a message to leave behind. Narcissistic to say the least. You had your chance when you were here, move on Dr. Ma thought. They just droned on about their life and circumstances excessively, as they so reluctantly left this plane of existence.

Dr. Ma always listened to the Winds that came with an important message. Information sent to her from humans she was here to protect. You had to give credit to the strength of emotion that a simple human could use to create a Spirit Wind. The Adepts, magicians and psychics, Dr. Ma expected to accomplish such a feat.

Bending the Universal energy into a moving entity like a Wind, even temporarily, was quite an accomplishment. It may be the last expenditure of energy the Spirit would make on this plane.

Dr. Ma was feeling more restored every step. She was full of the determination needed to do her part in rebalancing the negative energy from the young lady, who left her the images of a gruesome demise.

She took the turn south of Donald Trump's lovely Mar-a-Lago estate and looped north heading west again and home. Several cyclists passed on her left. One looked back and called out a greeting.

She recognized Scott Thomas, a patient recently back in the saddle after a fall. She smiled and waved. It was great, seeing her athletes whole and back to training for their next competition. Ma's practice specialty was Sports Medicine.

The battered face of the young woman she had just communed with about her death, came to mind. She would not be riding today. From what Dr. Ma was shown she had been a cyclist. That had been evident in the images of the crime scene shown to her.

Dr. Ma didn't recognize her. She probably wasn't local. Ma rode with the local cycling groups two evenings a week to give her body a change of pace from her morning runs. Plenty of cycling groups rode north to the end of Palm Beach Island from Ft. Lauderdale. Ma had even met some from Miami.

Dr. Ma would head home, shower and dress for work now, letting the visions the Spirit Wind brought process a bit. She would get together with David at some point in the day, between patients, and discuss what she saw. What they saw, actually. David's abilities had grown steadily. She knew he was able to 'see' a great deal of the Spirit's message.

Dr. Ma would have her assistant Winnie, call Detective Jeremy Brenner when she arrived at the office. Detective Brenner was Dr. Ma's contact in the Palm Beach Police Department. She wasn't sure about the jurisdiction of the murder, but Brenner would handle it.

At least Brenner didn't think of her as completely crazy. The thing was, how can you be crazy when you are exactly right? Unless of course you were the murderer, or an accomplice. Dr. Ma had given that some thought. Would there ever be a time when she couldn't show the police who were investigating one of her, *envisioned,* crimes that she clearly was not involved?

Hopefully never. That could be unpleasant. Lots of psychics helped police. Unfortunately she was not exactly like those psychics called upon to help locate bodies and clues. Ma called the police first. They did not call her. She knew everything about the crime, almost. It was up to the police to work out the details. Yep, more dangerous to be her.

So it began again. Another crime scene, another mystery. Those who would tell you that psychics, or something like her, could involve themselves in any event they choose, would be pulling your leg. The Universe points its finger.

We are all here for something, and often that something finds you. If you let it. If you can handle it. As Yoda said in Star Wars, "There is do or do not, there is no try."

Chapter Three - David At The Dojo

Long, corded muscle rippled as he moved. Slow then fast, up and down, in and out, as was the four point basis of all Tai Chi movements. Pausing it seemed in midair, he was an impossible feat of gravity.

Graceful, beautiful, and terrifying the Tai Chi students who watched thought silently. David quickly and easily demonstrated the section of form they were to learn this morning.

There were 15 students in class. The Mugen Dojo was a small martial arts school with a big reputation for high level training. The entire space was perfectly designed, with flexible wooden floors, gold medal level floor pads for falling, and an expensive array of practice weapons on the wall.

Moving faster and faster in the final moments, he seemed to explode with activity and then, as quickly as it came, the rapid attack of an imaginary opponent ceased. He slowed each limb in flawless sequence until he was completely still. His eyes half closed, even his facial muscles were in repose. His breathing, despite the recent flurry of movement, was quiet, almost imperceptible.

David smiled at them and asked if there were questions before they began training.

Who could have come up with a question? Experienced and new practitioners alike were usually speechless after his demos. In fact that is why he had a class waiting list and all the private lessons he could manage.

One student, new to class, clapped in spontaneous appreciation, until she noticed the other students were not joining her. David flashed his beautiful smile at her and bowed slightly to acknowledge her appreciation.

The young woman flushed as his smile touched a deep instinctual response in her. To her embarrassment she realized it was a sexual response to him. "First day in class and I have the hots for the teacher," she thought.

She looked around surreptitiously and noticed the majority of the students, female and some male, had poorly concealed looks of longing aimed at the gorgeous teacher standing in front of them as well.
"Ok," she thought, "its not just me." Still, embarrassing! "Keep it under control Gracie." David and Dr. Ma were the best teachers around hands down. She wanted to learn everything

she could from them. "Nothing is going to inter-fere with my Olympic dreams," she told herself. Except her mother.

Despite Gracie's wins in local and National competitions for the last several years, her mother remained unconvinced of her ability to make it into Olympic competition.

Her wrestling coach Lilly, a former Olympic wrestler and martial artist was convinced she had what it took. Gracie worked a part time job after school and trained tirelessly. "Since she paid for her own lessons, her mother wasn't go-ing to stop her. No matter what," she thought.

Gracie returned her attention to the front of the room. Davids upper body seemed barely cov-ered by a thin material of basic black. Some short sleeved, sweat wicking t-shirt, that al-lowed the movement of muscle to be clearly observed.

The elastic leggings covering his lower body, left nothing to the imagination. That was the point. Not to titillate, although it surely did that for those who were interested.

The point of close fitting clothing was to show the student in detail what was happening as the teacher moved through the form.

For a long time Tai Chi outfits were long and flowing. Students and teachers alike in the USA, bought this gear and wore it religiously. The long flowing gear however, wasn't meant to be a visual barrier between the teacher and their students. It was meant to be a visual barrier between the teacher, their chosen students, and outsiders.

Outsiders such as the teacher and students of a rival school.
Flowing outfits masked the subtlety of movement when forms were on public display, such as in a competition.

When the teacher and students were inside the school and away from prying eyes that were trying to divulge their fighting secrets, the instructor would teach in closer fitting gear to expose the delicate and often missed underlying movements.

In fact, David and Dr. Ma would direct the more serious students, to closely observe the harmony of opposites as one group of muscles moved, assisted by the contraction of the opposing group. Dr. Ma and David both boasted elegant and visible muscle structures making this lesson in observation closer to watching moving art.

Dr. Ma always appeared to be a moving, breathing ice sculpture when she taught. Flawless and cool, hardly breaking a sweat. David appeared more like an out of control wildfire, radiating heat. His perfect body always displayed a glistening sheen of perspiration.

He was intense. She was intimidating.
.
If you arrived early for class when he was practicing forms on his own, you would see him, often bare to the waist, a small pair of snug workout shorts and a man's best friend, the supportive cup under them, as his only garments.

Like any elite athlete, he would train for hours in combinations of extreme difficulty. He would run and workout in the outdoor training area at the school. Afterward, he would practice forms on the dojo floor.

Dr. Ma, David and Sosam Li, a student of theirs, had built the school's outdoor training area. It was traditional, a wood gallery of physical challenges resembling the Ninja Warrior competitions so popular on TV these days.

David did use running shoes outside, to avoid leaving too much of his skin on the hot pavement. Any other time he was barefoot. Unlike Dr. Ma, David was not a cyclist. His fitness came from the martial arts.

David's lower abdomen and waist, around to his buttocks, bore unique tattoos. Strange symbols and slivers of gems just under the skin of his ripped lower abdomen were a source of fascination for anyone who saw them. Graceful vine like branches and leaves wound around his hips, diving down his buttocks on either side.

Such beautiful skin, a golden tan with vibrant tattoo colors and… were those scars? Yes, it seemed like there were along his upper back, here and there, fine lines, jagged sometimes. Definitely scars, but from what, people would think who saw them?

Nobody knew the origins of the tattoos, or the scars, in class. They weren't likely to find out either. You could ask David anything and get either a breathtakingly honest answer or a polite refusal to answer. When it came to the tattoos, the polite refusal was always in place.

As David moved among the practicing students, Gracie noticed a light sheen of sweat covered his glowing skin. The skin that appeared to be perfectly adhered to the underlying rippling muscles. There was no layer of fat or fluid between the two. She bit her tongue sharply to refocus her attention on the form. "Get it together, or change to only Dr. Ma's classes," she told herself sharply.

Gracie was not David's only admirer, Sosam Li was watching his beloved instructor move from student to student assessing their form. He was fascinated by David's facial features. Sharp cheekbones below lapis blue eyes. Who had that color eyes? Many students and patients had gotten lost in those eyes.

There was no heavy or labored breathing from David despite his recent gravity defying leaps, kicks and turns. His cardiovascular fitness level was legendary even among Dr. Ma's athlete clientele. Some of Ma's fastest and best had given up trying to outdo him. What confused them most, was his lack of interest in competition.

Samuel Lightner, a world class ultra marathoner ran with David whenever he was in town to see Dr. Ma.

"Come on man," he would say to David. "Run Northern States with me this year. I could use the company."

"And the challenge?" David would reply. "Are you sure you want to feel bad about me keeping pace with you?"

Sam was about to celebrate forty two years of age. Most of it had been spent running and competing. The last ten years, he seemed to be winning every Ultra title he could manage.

"Sign up and let see if you can," Sam retorted.

"I don't see color," David grinned. "As long as the start and finish lines have the words written as well as the trail markers, I will be fine."

He didn't see colors, so he didn't drive a car either. Dr. Ma or Winnie usually drove or he walked, ran or took public transportation. He was color blind of course, like all tigers were, and had somewhat less than optimal vision in daylight. At night his vision was profound. So much so that it was distracting. Best not to drive unless needed.

"Stick with me and you won't get lost," Sam said. "Pass me at the finish line, if you make it that far."

Sam and many other athletes knew David's speed and endurance from first hand experience. Sam was pretty sure David could leave him during the race and probably beat the whole field easily. It was almost inhuman.

David's students had been known to wonder if he was human when training them. Then there was the 100 watt smile and easy sexuality that tempted some to think they would gladly find out how human he actually was. Like Gracie.

Both Dr. Ma and David were well known in the local martial arts community. That is how Gracie had learned of them.

She had attended a competition where Dr. Ma did a weapons demonstration and David did one for Tai Chi. Their Mugen Dojo had underwritten the competition and there was a host of schools and students that couldn't have afforded to attend otherwise. It was free.

Gracie had never seen so many martial arts students in one place with their teachers. It was overwhelming and inspiring. Dr. Ma and David had quite a few students in the competition, but the judges were Asian and from nowhere local. To keep things fair.

After the competition, Gracie had gone by the Mugen Dojo to observe the two teaching. David and Dr. Ma's classes were interesting mixes of true practitioners, wide eyed newbies interested in the sport, and, of course, students interested in the sexy teacher. David, that is.

"Gracie stop it!" she had thought. She gave herself a break on the slight crush. If that is why his students attended, well, we all come to the path of enlightenment by varying routes. Don't we?

The front door of the school opened silently, leaving a slice of bright sunlight to split the room of students in half. Dr. Ma stood there without speaking while the students jumped up to acknowledge her. A row of deep bows, from the waist were performed almost in unison. Proper respect, shown to the senior instructor of the school.

The Mugen Dojo. The school without limits. In naming the school, Dr. Ma and David had meant a multi-layered Asian perspective on *no personal limits*. The students would decide the limits in their learning.

David noticed Dr. Ma was oddly dressed for this time of day in tight training pants and a short sleeve wicking t-shirt like his own. She carried her favorite bokken. Ash was her choice of composition for the weapon. Bokken was the name of the wood, not steel version of a Japanese training sword.

"Joining class?" he inquired silently.

"For a few minutes," she replied just as silently.

David grinned and waved his students off the dojo floor. The class had remained standing, but now moved to the west wall in a line, to be capable of observing both of them.

David's grin was infectious. The class immediately realized they were in for a rare exhibition between the two masters. Even Dr. Ma smiled, briefly.

As Ma moved forward suddenly and without warning, David executed a backflip, landing and leaping to the east side where all the training weapons were hung in rows.

Ma immediately re-directed and swept the bokken in a wide arc, narrowly missing David's midsection.

The students tried to contain any sounds out of respect and a false attempt at emotional control, but gasps of surprise were still audible. Full on demonstrations from these two were very rare, but it never seemed like either was holding back at all. You always expected blood.

The bokken rotated it's cutting blade almost like magic in Ma's hands and returned along the first arc. There was an audible 'whooshing' sound from the speed and strength of the intended blow.

David crouched and rolled to avoid the second cut. He sprang up pulling another bokken from the wall and immediately charged into Ma's opening from her last movement.

Ma turned her horizontal bottom right hand over the supporting left hand, effectively changing the wooden blades cutting surface again. Dipping her left shoulder, she brought the blade upward from its last position and into David's oncoming downward strike.

The crack of the wooden blades seemed thunderous in the small, quiet room. The students were all but holding their collective breaths.

Neither combatant gave an inch with the powerful contact. In fact, they both grinned and laughed. Backing up, both transferred the bokken to their left and right hands to indicate the conflict had ended.
Dr. Ma was right handed and David was left handed. Placing the weapon into the opposite hand of the former striking one, was how you indicated no further attack would be forthcoming.

The students remained still and standing, but the smiles on their faces revealed their fascination and enjoyment.

Dr. Ma and David bowed to each other and then the class of students. David replaced his bokken on the training wall and Ma carried hers towards the back door. She had to get to work and the dojo back door opened near to the clinic back door for convenience.

David was getting the students onto the training floor as she quietly left.

Dr. Ma took a deep breath in the attached Zen garden behind the two businesses. It was going to be a beautiful south Florida day. For some. The sudden flurry of violent activity had cleared that primal part of her mind. One that didn't change from manifestation to manifestation. She was, deep down, a quiet and thoughtful predator. Not one of those who would wreak pain and suffering on others. The brief attack mockup with David help quell her instinctive desire to open her pair of powerful dragon's jaws, grip the man who had killed that lovely girl with her vicious back foot talons and tear his head off.

She moved forward to the small fountain of rock in the center left of the garden. A smiling Buddha sat there with an open burlap sack at his feet.

In Buddhism, he was known as Hotei. His visage was based on the stories of an eccentric Zen monk who lived over 1,000 years ago. David and Dr. Ma followed similar paths, Chinese in origin, she Taoist, he, more a Buddhist.

The little burlap sack was given a fresh offering of fruit daily. Dr. Ma knew the birds and lizards who could enter the tiny slats of the garden enclosure ate them. They were gone every morning.

Hotei himself would have been happy that the tiny creatures benefited from his daily spiritual gift. In fact Ma was sure he would. They had known each other for a brief time.

Under the small plate of fresh fruit the sack held an array of goods that Hotei would have carried with him. Rice plants, candy for children and the woes of the world he picked up along the way, were what was supposed to be represented.

Dr. Ma closed her eyes in front of the small statue. The delicate tinkling of water falling below him, blended with the buzz of local bees in her orchid flowers, and the tiny voices of small birds calmed her as they flitted in and out of the enclosed garden area.

A deep meditative breath cleared the emotional debris of her mind and clarified the facts of the crime. She was ready to hunt him. The killer. She was calm.

"Ah well," thought Dr. Ma, as she opened the back door of her clinic. "The killer will be better off with me just helping to catch him." She flashed briefly to the image of her snapping dragon's jaws removing his head cleanly. "He just doesn't know he'll be better off."

Chapter Four - Winnie At The Zen Clinic

The backdoor chime pulled Winnie Chelasko's focus out of today's patient files. The wall clock showed 8:30 AM. Already? Winnie knew that Dr. Ma would have been up since 4:30 AM. It was her daily habit. She liked to run along the Intracoastal Waterway in the wee hours and think.

Winnie expected Dr. Ma at promptly 8:55 AM every morning. Ma would walk in, nod hello, leave her briefcase and donning a lab coat and head to Room One for the first patient of the day.

"The woman is a model of efficiency," Winnie thought. "If Dr. Ma is here early, something unusual must have happened." Winnie was used to unusual, after years in Dr. Ma's employ.

"Good morning, Winnie," Dr. Ma said. "Would you see if you can get Detective Brenner on the phone?"

"Yes, Dr. Ma," Winnie responded. Then she added "Good morning!" as Dr. Ma disappeared back down the hall to her private office to prepare for the day of patients.

"Oh, good," Winnie thought, "another mystery!" As she picked up the phone to dial it quickly dawned on her that this mystery probably went hand in hand with a sad circumstance for someone. "Try not to be so happy about it then, Winifred," she chided herself. Her mother's tone of voice always seemed the choice when she was self correcting. Winnie sighed and left a message for Detective Brenner on his answering machine.

As the back door chime rang again Winnie looked up to see Dr. David Anderson following Dr. Ma by just minutes. Now Winnie knew something was going on. David would have just finished his Tai Chi class. They must have quit a few minutes early. Very unlike David. Not that the man wasn't already many hours into his day like Dr. Ma.

Winnie knew his morning routine was a crazy fast 10 mile run along A1A in Palm Beach, finishing at their clinic in West Palm Beach. David had lived in Palm Beach since she knew him. He would then put in least 60 minutes of personal martial arts training. The 30 minutes of Tai Chi training that followed was a brief advanced student class in the dojo next door.

The Tai Chi class should still be going on, probably with the doctors' teaching assistant Jet Carlson. Jet also taught Qigong. Their teaching assistant for karate was Sosam Li.

Only Dr. Ma taught the weapons classes. She had no assistant other than David. David or Dr. Ma would just demonstrate form the first 30 minutes then leave them to practice 30 more.

David almost bounded into the room when he arrived. He was thirty years younger than Winnie in theory. She always thought that she was the Energizer bunny rabbit until she met David. She envied his stamina.

She didn't envy his sweaty clothing and body after training. She swore he smelled like one of her three cats, Hugo, when he got wet standing with her in the shower each morning.

Dr. Ma had a private staff shower and bath installed in the clinic with David in mind. Ma showered at home. David came in sweaty. Also, too sexy in tight fitting Tai Chi gear, in Winnie's opinion to be seen by the patients.

"Winifred! No thinking your employer was sexy," she thought Winnie was over sixty but she wasn't dead yet! Winnie always gave David a full 30 minutes to, well, shower and change into 'decent' clothing.

Dr. Ma always smiled at Winnie's facial expression when David came in early to work, sweat melting his thin running gear onto an impressive physique. Winnie never realized she made that church lady, pinched lip expression, until Dr. Ma had pointed it out to her.

David stopped in Dr. Ma's office doorway smiling and sweating. Ma knew this was the second big sweat of the day. During his morning run he probably clocked an average sub 5 minute mile. David was fast and fit. At 35, or so his medical license said, he was beyond stunning.

Dr. Ma knew how old he really was. Not this body he was in, though. This body was really thirty five years old.

"Winnie is getting in touch with Detective Brenner. Hopefully he can join us for lunch" Dr. Ma said.

"Better get to the body before the evidence is scattered by scavengers in that type of location," David replied.

So, David had 'seen' the location too. Ma was pleased that David's abilities had been expanding over the last couple centuries to include Sight. *Sight* was the ability to visualize a Spirit's message in real time.

At almost 6'5, David sported a ponytail of thick, wavy, sun streaked, blond hair. Unbound, it would come to just below shoulder length. He tied it up during the clinic workday for cleanliness and a clear field of vision. Winnie often remarked that it was a matter of being professional.

Winnie's own thinner, straight, salt and pepper locks were always pulled back in a tight bun.

David's intense gaze showed the unique eye color that matched Dr. Ma's. "We all had those odd lapis blue eyes if you knew what to look for," she thought. "Elementals of course. Something in the transition gave us all those same color eyes when we manifest as humans."

Ma thought back to another tiger she had known so long ago. A thousand years apart and she still thought of him every day. Where was he now, the soul matched spirit to hers? Tigers and Dragons in Chinese mythology were complete opposites, yet inextricably bound, like Yin and Yang.

They had been together for the first millennia of both his and her existence. She thought about David. Almost the same amount of time we have been together. Am I destined to lose a companion every thousand years or so?

"Hello?" David said breaking her train of thought.

Dr. Ma realized she had left David hanging outside of her inner conversation. Only she, could do that to him. He couldn't lock her out of his thoughts. He was almost childlike and quite genuine, certainly capable of physical violence with his strength and endurance. He, however, was not the one who projected an ever present aura of danger.
That was Ma. Dr. Ma, older than he and from where, David had never known exactly. He knew she had been created as all air creatures were. He had been born from the earth. He usually felt gentle to human senses where she often triggered fear.

David only caused a fear reaction from humans in intimate situations.

They had known each other most of David's life this time around. The fact that both of them partnered for each re-manifestation was a contract so old neither really knew the origin. Not that it mattered. Coming back was a choice.

David smiled his 100 watt smile and said,"So, Boss, how was your run this morning?"

"Funny man," she responded, cocking her head to the side and giving him a somewhat comical look. Her raised eyebrows wiggled slightly and he burst out laughing. "Sorry," he said, "That may have been in poor taste."

"Not at all! But really, thanks for the help." She was appreciative, of course.

"Something was off about this one," David said, a slight frown marring his usually smooth forehead.

"I agree. Did you catch that unusual smell?" she asked. Ma placed emphasis on the word *unusual*, indicating that it was strange because they didn't expect it to be there.

"Yes," he agreed nodding imperceptibly. He was of the same opinion evidently. It had been an otherworldly presence smell. Not much more than that, yet.

"Funny man," she said again this time with a different meaning. "I can still taste the metallic blood residue from the air. Then there was that oddly foul smell. I am thinking something non-human involved. The event was fresh, but something smelled decayed."

"Yes, it was nice," David said wrinkling his nose."Well, isn't that why we are here? For the random other worldly murderers? I assume this will be a lunchtime discussion?" he asked.

"Yes. Hopefully with Brenner. I think we need to start on this one tonight though, the scene is unprotected and the body was moved," she replied. "Wait, you smelled the decay from my Spirit Wind?" Dr. Ma said with surprise.

"Yes," David agreed grinning. He was getting stronger lately, able to pick up on ethereal things during Dr. Ma's Wind vision that he never had before. "Maybe it was the location and hu-midity. What was it this morning, eighty degrees at 5:00 AM? I love January in South Florida."

Dr. Ma actually loved the heat and the heavy sweating from training in it. All those toxins accumulating from the environment just poured out leaving you fresh and clean. "It certainly is toasty for this time of year. Global warming I assume."

"Gab session time is up," Winnie said, entering the office,shooing Dr. Ma in the direction of the patient rooms. "You," she said pointing at David, "hit the shower. You didn't get here early enough to dawdle. Detective Brenner said he would be here for lunch if we order from the Thai place."

"Ugh!" David contributed. He was raw vegan and the Thai restaurant that Brenner preferred was more of an American sugar/carb food combination than healthy and clean food.

"We will treat," Ma nodded at Winnie and pre- pared to head to Room One for her first patient appointment of the day. Dr. Ma saw twelve to fifteen patients in a normal workday. Her area of specialization was acupuncture while David's specialty was Tui'na. Dr. Ma's highly refined sense of energetic flow allowed her to deter- mine treatment with uncanny accuracy.

Winnie nodded her agreement on the treating for lunch. No reason to ask what they wanted. Ma was steamed veggies and black rice no sauce. David was raw veggies and soaked rice also no sauce.

Winnie patted her as usual severe hairstyle and gifted them with her patented 'serious business' expression.

Knowing her well, Dr. Ma knew that expression to be Winnie's version of either a delightful early morning greeting, or a nudge to go into the patients room and get on with the work that awaited them.

Winnie grunted and pointed her finger at David.

"Is there a shower and change of clothes in your future or should we call the Chippendale's audition committee?"

David favored her with one of his blinding smiles and practically disappeared, he slipped away so quickly down the hallway.

"He just takes his time getting going in the morning, huh?" Winnie said to Dr. Ma.

Ma knew Winnie loved David, and it seemed that their bantering back and forth, had given Winnie a new purpose in life. David joining the practice a couple years after Ma had started it and hired Winnie, seemed to have given the older woman someone to mother, or rather harass, into Winnie's idea of an upstanding young physician.

Winnie also had a husband, children and grandchildren but it seemed she had energy to spare to whip David into shape. Metaphorically speaking, of course.

David was a perfect project for Winnie. He was casual where she was strict. He was forgetful in business matters, as she was organized. She tweaked the tiniest detail to perfection.

Dr. Ma pulled the patient chart out of the holder next to the door of Room One and walked in. Winnie shook her head and walked back to rule their world from the front desk.

Dr. Ma had been Winnie's boss for thirteen years, still, Winnie felt she didn't know her at all. Ma was always self contained, intense and said very little.

Ma always expected a lot, yet was very hands off in the day to day operation of the clinic. She let Winnie run the business aspects of the practice as she saw fit. The only stipulation was that everything ran smoothly and efficiently.

Winnie and David knew and respected the odd 'presence' that Ma had in dealing with just about everything. She commanded respect without effort. In intense situations her direct and unwavering gaze combined with near silence could strike a chill of fear in anyone.

Fit and attractive there was an undeniable sense of an ancient mind residing in Ma's head. She had a distinct 'otherness' about her, especially in difficult situations.

Winnie often was working late when David and Ma taught classes and would take their meditation or beginner Tai Chi classes.

Coming into the practice an out of shape, unhealthy, disbeliever in all things not conventional, she had made many changes.

Winnie met Dr. Ma twenty years prior and they had struck up a solid friendship. Winnie was a top notch personal shopper at a high end department store. Ma needed someone to handle her wardrobe efficiently. Dr. Ma was invited to quite a few social events every year and had little interest in acquiring or curating her closet. She did, however, have a strong flair for fashion.

Enter Winifred Chelasko, atelier extraordinaire. She not only arranged for the incredible makeover the local California Closet store had done for one of Dr. Ma's spare rooms turning it into a super organized dressing room and closet, but then had filled it with coordinated items.

Of course it all went on Dr. Ma's credit card and Winnie made the commission. This was probably when Winnie's husband Bud, first fell in love with Dr. Ma. The second time was after he ate her incredible food when they visited for dinner.

When Dr. Ma then asked Winnie to come work for her it ended up being a productive partnership. Effectively, it got Winnie out of a retail sales life that was becoming more and more difficult for the older woman and gave Dr. Ma a fiercely loyal and efficient office manager.

There wasn't a soul who, either was treated at Dr. Ma's practice, delivered goods there, or attended a class in the Mugen Dojo, that didn't seem to love Winnie.

All the love of course tinged with a healthy dose of fear and respect. The older woman was indeed a force to be reckoned with. If everything went her way, all was well. There wasn't really another option. "Why should there be?" Winnie would say. Everything was working well in the world according to Winnie.

No need for change.

Winnie gave out 'sweeties' and 'dears' like Halloween candy. She peppered every conversation with endearments and personalizations.

She knew your birthday, anniversary, pet's name and kept current on your last conversation with her the next time you met. Even years later. It was odd to say the least.

David made his appearance in the reception area post shower and flawlessly attired in Brooks Brothers suit pants and a custom tailored shirt (no tie), just as his middle aged female patient pulled open the front door.

He smiled his signature smile at the attractive woman. Fixing her gaze on his handsome face, she smiled, and just kept going past Winnie's sign in sheet on the front desk.

As usual, Winnie thought, and headed her off. She gave David a disapproving frown over her shoulder. "There is a call on line one for you Dr. Anderson," she lied to get him out of the way while she got the patient properly settled.

"Mrs. Diamonte," Winnie stepped in front of her and gently turned her back to the desk. "Dr. Anderson will be right with you dear, now just sign in and then have a seat,"….Winnie trailed off giving David her raised eyebrow look indicating again that he should make himself scarce until she let him know the patient was ready.

David ducked into his office off the main hall smiling at her. "You are a royal pain in my ass," Winnie thought. "It's bad enough your patient's tend to moon over you, but then you muck up my organization of the reception area by just showing up when they first get here." She would have a little chat with him later about this. Again.

Meanwhile, Dr. Ma was wading her way through a new patient evaluation in Room One.

He was the father of an existing patient of hers. His son was a world class tennis player. John, the father, was in his eighties and on so much medication it took up 5 pages of his medical history form. He had it typed out for her. She decided John would make a great patient for David.

Dr. Ma somehow managed the 90 minute evaluation, to get him started on a recovery plan, and moved on to her next appointment.

Dr. Ma was a legendary healer. Patients who had just met her were invariably astonished at her rapid assessments and even more rapid results. She would tell you that what she actually excelled at was initial diagnosis. Treating only the patients she could do so successfully, she felt added to her, reputation.

David, on the other hand, was the master of Tui'na, the manual therapy portion of Traditional Chinese Medicine. They made a great pair from a practice standpoint. If the treatment course would be better served with the other's specialty, they were right there in the office to transition the patient.

Both were profound herbalists. That was never a concern regardless of whom the patient may see first. With the globalization of alternative medicine practice, even acquiring high quality raw herbs was a simple process. Dr. Ma remembered when the two of them would go and search fields and markets to stock their pharmacy shelves.

That was at least a hundred years ago or so. Dr. Ma appreciated the ease of Internet ordering today.

She passed David in the hall, as he was saying goodbye to Mrs. Diamonte.

"Thank you so much Dr. Anderson," Mrs. Diamonte cooed, touching David's arm as he walked her down the hall. "I can't believe how much better I am feeling these days under your care."

David turned to find Ma giving him her most mischievous grin. He walked back down the hallway with her.

"Such powerful healing magic you have young Jedi," she teased.

"If I could have this type of success so simply with all my patients I would take it," David replied grinning back.

Fifteen patients were on the schedule today with complaints ranging from acute injury to migraine headaches. There was no accounting for the walk-ins or last minutes and of course any sports related emergencies.

Dr. Ma and David specialized in Sports Medicine as it applied to Traditional Chinese Medicine. Both were Board Certified. Only Dr. Ma had completed her doctorate (again). David was working diligently on his. Ma could teach the classes eyes and ears closed. The problem was that it was hard to move licenses and certifications not only through lifetimes but in varying locations.

The issues associated with interminable lifetimes increased every year with the digital tracking and Internet access now provided. Unlike the welcome improvement in acquiring herbs, this was less than welcome. Dr. Ma had a Allistair's small professional company, that handled everything for her and David. Their wealth and property was maintained for them through all of their re-manifestations.

Their human forms could, would, and should die eventually but it wasn't easy to kill them. Especially, David. He hadn't lived quite as long as Dr Ma but he was nearly indestructible. Good, now that he was in grad school.

Enjoying the classes once a month, this would be David's first doctoral degree. He was still taking one week a month to complete his studies in Fort Lauderdale at the Trans Pacific Institute for Traditional Chinese Medicine, her alma mater. It was difficult to get a doctorate in Chinese Medicine in the USA with only 4 official programs in the country.

Not that doctoral degrees were common. Their field payed little. No more money was made with a doctoral degree, just debt paid out. For Dr. Ma and David, this was more about doing something to keep their minds busy.

They had no real need for money Their income could be high or low without effecting their lifestyle or needs. After millennia of existence, there was plenty. No small thanks due to Dr. Ma's private solicitor Allistair McGowan.

Allistair was an otherworldly being that Dr. Ma had entrusted her entire legal and financial affairs to. He worked for other entities, of course, including himself, via his firm Ouroboros International Law and Trust. An ouroboros was an ancient symbol of a serpent consuming their own tail in an endless circle of rejuvenation. How appropriate for the Elemental water snake he was.

Allistair also opened a local practice wherever Dr. Ma and David settled and had located this time in Miami. The smaller adjunct law firm was titled simply McGowan and McGowan. Dr. Ma knew it was an inside joke of Allistair's that he was two different McGowans. One was the staid and conservative attorney, the other, well, a rather intimidating otherworldly being.

Picking up another patient chart outside of the treatment room and entering, Dr. Ma greeted the young man who was waiting for her. "Hello Scott," Dr. Ma said entering Room Three. "Didn't I see you riding this morning?"

"Morning Doc!" Scott Thomas replied smiling. Scott had just gotten back to competitive cycling after a bad accident on A1A a few months ago. Between Dr. David and Dr. Ma, he didn't know if he would have even been able to compete again.

An older woman in a small white sedan had gone through the red light at A1A and Lake Worth Road. She was southbound and Scott had been turning north from eastbound lane of Lake Worth Road.

The elderly lady had just kept going between the stopped cars on the right getting ready to go west over the Lake Worth Bridge and the stopped cars on the left preparing to turn east up to the Lake Worth Beach parking and Casino Shops. Scott never saw her until it was too late. She lifted him and his bike up and over her hood, cracking the windshield, and kept driving.

The Town of Gulfstream Police Department had finally stopped her driving, south, through their jurisdiction. She still had a piece of his shattered carbon fiber road bike frame wedged into the area between her front bumper and and front grill.

Witnesses to the accident stayed with Scott and blocked the area until Emergency Medical personnel arrived. The first person Scott called when he got to the hospital was Dr. Ma. She had met him there and gone over all his test results. The best news for Scott had been when she told him the worst that had happened was needing a new bike.

Dr. Ma finished her last followup on Scott, testing his range of motion, assessing his muscle recovery and asking general questions about his health and well being. "Well, Scott, we should be good here," she said. "Make sure you set up a monthly wellness appointments with Winnie before you leave."

"Yes, Doc, and thank you so much," Scott gave her a brief hug. "I can't thank you, enough."

Dr. Ma smiled and hugged him back and moved on to Room Two. "Hello Emily," Dr. Ma greeted Emily Lightner. "I see you have the cold going around," she said as Emily sneezed into a wad of crumpled Kleenex. She was Samuel Lightner's wife, a good friend of David's. She was also an open water swimmer, unlike her husband, who was an ultra distance runner.

Despite their specialty in Sports Medicine they seemed to have a broad-based practice ranging from their competitive athlete patients to the extended family of said athletes. Colds, arthritis, weight loss, and more seemed to crop up on a daily basis with their non sports patients.

Dr. Ma took a quick pulse and tongue assessment even though she could see and hear the obvious signs of an upper respiratory infection. "Based on everything you told me and what I am seeing here Emily, I have a granular tea that should improve your symptoms significantly."

"Thank you Dr. Ma. I'm training pretty hard lately for some upcoming events. I don't want this to hang in too long," Emily replied blowing her nose loudly.

"No training for two to three, days and that means sleeping, drinking and eating like you are on vacation," Dr. Ma replied. "That was not a suggestion," she continued with a slight frown.

They both laughed knowing that it was never easy to get one of the clinic's competitive athletes to relax a few days to recover from illness. They were all so used to pushing through pain and discomfort from training, there was little differentiation when internal imbalance was the problem. Dr. Ma was always grateful these problem children hardly ever got sick.

Dr. Ma and David breezed through the rest of the morning. Lunch would be a welcome respite, even if they were talking about murder with Detective Brenner. They had a full afternoon of appointments.

David popped his head around Dr. Ma's partly open office door. "Almost lunch time," he said. David was always hungry.

Like most high level athletes,their metabolisms burned a lot of calories but both ran rapidly. There were also other reasons for their calorie burning capabilities.

"Hungry young one?" Dr. Ma inquired smiling knowingly. David's stomach growled in response.

David flashed back to the first meal he had shared with Ma. They had just met, literally, and found they would be paired together by their all knowing creators.

They had found several demons decimating a small village. A quick but decisive battle ended up Ma and David three, to demons zero. The creatures killed half the village it appeared, by the amount of blood on the ground. There were no bodies left. They were eaten, most likely, by the demons.

It had been a local festival day pre demon arrival. The tables had been heaped with various food dishes. The demons would only have been interested in the villagers as food. Ma and David needed human food to maintain the strength in their non Elemental bodies.

Not ones to waste perfectly good food and since they were the only two left that appeared to be interested in eating, they sat down and filled their bellies. They left the rest for the wild animals and any villages who had managed to flee in time.

Dr. Ma brought David's attention back to the present by saying, "I have one more patient and then I will join you, don't touch my food."

David grinned and disappeared around the door frame. "Wait," Dr. Ma called after him. "I will need you on this one." David reappeared and opened the door fully for her to walk out in the hall. Ma pulled the chart out of the door hanger and walked into Room Four with David in tow.

Her next patient was a world class endurance trail runner with an odd complaint. David's last morning patient had rescheduled until the afternoon, so she called him in to consult.

"I am having rectal pain while running but only after fifty miles or so. It lasts sometimes a few hours and sometimes a few minutes," the patient told them.

"Have you tried the sitting roll technique I showed you with the Trigger Point GRID Roller?" Ma asked.

"Yes," he replied, "twice daily. It worked well for a while, but now it is back with a vengeance."

"Have you ever fallen on your tailbone?" Ma asked.

"Yes, I didn't remember it the last time I saw you, but my mother reminded me, that I fell off one of those bouncing rubber balls with the handle when I was growing up."

Ma looked at David and nodded smiling. " All yours," she said, and excused herself from the room.

The patient looked at David inquisitively, "Dr. Anderson?"

David grimaced slightly and said, "Probably a mildly deviated coccyx. I am going to have to do a non invasive manipulation to help resolve it."

The patient watched David wash his hands and put protective rubber gloves on. There was no mistaking how Dr. Anderson was going to effect that treatment resolution. In reality it was simple and painless.

The gloves were for general sanitation as David gently manipulated the coccygeal bone from the surface below the sacrum. After a tiny 'pop' the patient noticed a distinct sensation of no more pressure and pain relief.

David walked him out with his chart and told him to return if the pain returned but to have hope that this was going to be the resolution to his discomfort.

The front door opened ringing the wind chimes on the tension arm as Dr. Ma set her last patient chart of the morning on Winnie's desk.

Detective Jeremy Brenner entered from the brilliant sun-washed walkway to the dimly lit inside, blinking his eyes to get them to adjust.

He saw Dr. Ma and smiled. "Thai?" Brenner asked hopefully.

Ma nodded. "Of course." She knew his dietary preference whether she agreed with it or not. He was fit and healthy enough at this moment. We all had to choose our path, even if it came paved with crappy food.

"Extra greasy ribs with that sticky sauce, starchy dumplings and a sugar filled soda on its way," Winnie said from behind the file area. The front desk in the reception room was a massive affair with a chest high marble arc, starting at the front door and encompassing Winnie's domain, but for a small walk through for the doctors.

There were plenty of elegant wicker and rattan seating options with red and gold hues intermingled with the entire spectrum of the color green in silk plants. This relaxed area was for patients. Not, Winnie.

Behind the front desk, Winnie's domain was perfectly ordered, files stacked on floor to ceiling sliding file cabinets, dividing the space behind, which served as the doctors pharmacy area.

You wouldn't know it was a pharmacy area unless you walked back there which, of course, Winnie would never permit. Besides, it was against HIPPA and any other law or convention Winnie could bring into play to keep it isolated. As it should be.

The pharmacy itself was a spotless, sterile vision in white and stainless steel. Another masterful design by Winnie, courtesy of California Closets.

Two stainless work tables had scales, counting and measuring implements and reference books. Three walls of shelves with raw, dry, powdered, encapsulated, liquid and ointment based herbs and formulas made it the best stocked pharmacy around.

It would be the envy of other practitioners had they ever had the chance to see it. Dr. Ma and David worked alone, for many necessary reasons. They both shared their knowledge by teaching in Fort Lauderdale at Dr. Ma's alma mater. The head of the school, Dr. Chan, was typically Chinese when it came to saving money for the school. The fact that neither Dr. Ma or David accepted compensation for their work made her very happy.

The front door opened again. A smiling male worker from Joy's Happy Noodle Thai Restaurant entered with a stack of bagged takeout containers.

"Sawatdi," he said looking at Dr. Ma. He bowed from the waist, his palms pressed together like he was praying. The height he held this hands almost in front of his forehead noted the level of respect he showed her.

Dr. Ma was a frequent customer of Joy's. She and David were also well known to the local

Thai Buddhist priests who ate weekly at Joy's restaurant.

"Sawatdi, Kha," Dr. Ma replied lightly touching her palms together with a slight nod of her head.

The man repeated his greeting to David who made a similar nod and responded in kind "Sawatdi, Krup," David said. David to all appearances was at least a decade younger than the restaurant employee despite his status as a physician. They were using the traditional Thai greeting or 'wai.'

Detective Brenner and Winnie watched all this with interest but they were not included in the delivery man's greeting.

Winnie stepped forward to exchange the bag of food for a generous tip and the man left smiling as she locked the front door for their lunchtime break.

"I have to spend more time around you two" Detective Brenner said. "I have so much I want to learn about Asian cultures."

"You just want a free meal," Winnie joked. "Now sit down everyone and eat. "I imagine you have a lot to discuss, and I want to hear the details. Besides, I am starving."

Chapter Five - Dr. Ma Reveals A Murder

"So who died?" Detective Brenner asked, happily stuffing Joy's dumplings in his mouth and washing them down with a Coca Cola.

"I don't know her personally," Ma replied. "I do know she was a cyclist and I am sure I know where to find the body."

"We need to get to her sooner than later," David interjected. "Your crime scene and body are going to deteriorate quickly. She is on a marshy island outcropping half in and half out of the water."

Dr. Ma looked at him. David realized he had interrupted her in his excitement. It was rude but she would forgive him. "Sorry," he mouthed softly. Brenner hadn't heard that exchange over the joyful eating noises he was making. He loved Thai food.

"Great," Brenner replied, no pause in his chewing. He moved on to the beef ribs. They were so well done they practically fell apart when you picked them up. He was, after all, a homicide detective. Nothing really put him off his food. Detective Brenner was a good eater with a high metabolism, or he would wear the typical paunch of most busy detectives. "I can't wait to work a murder case with you two again. It certainly won't be normal," he said.

When there was no immediate reply from either Dr. Ma or David, Brenner looked up and raised both eyebrows in an unasked question. He quickly wondered whether his enthusiasm to work the case had been misinterpreted for not caring that someone had been murdered.

Sandy, ginger hair, was close cropped to a nicely shaped head. Brenner's light blue eyes, freckles, and an easy smile, combined with his friendly and personable demeanor, helped to make him a successful investigator.

Jeremy Brenner had trained with Dr. Ma and David for some years now in various martial arts disciplines and had the hard physique to prove it. He had always been into sports when he was in school and had never let himself go when he got into law enforcement. At 6', 180 pounds, Brenner was physically intimidating, when he needed to be.

His easy personality was just the door opener when he was into an investigation. Underneath, the man was a tenacious pit bull. He never let go of something, worrying his prey until it gave up. He could easily work for an agency that had a high rate of homicides, but he liked Palm Beach Police Department.

If his workload was light, Brenner was often lent to other agencies. Hi workload was very often light, in Palm Beach. He had a suspiciously high success rate in violent crime. Especially in homicides.

Much of his success was due to Dr. Ma and David, but he kept that under wraps. Police agencies were not new to using psychics, but Dr. Ma did not exactly fit in that category. She knew as much as the bad guy. Not so easily explained to his colleagues in law enforcement.

Detective Brenner stuffed the last bit of spicy, sauce laden rib meat in his mouth and looked over to Winnie. She was watching him out of the corner of her eye. He knew she liked him, just not his table manners.

Winnie was sitting in her corner of the reception couch with her meal, quiet, but all ears. She never knew this murder solving stuff was part of the job. It was always so interesting!

Winnie liked a good mystery novel as much as anyone else. Working here and almost being in the story, beat reading one any day. She, of course, shared nothing outside the office about their investigations, even to her beloved husband, Bud. He would never understand.

The man worried about her driving home each day. She had to text him when she left so he could gauge when she should be home. It was nice to be such a priority to him after all these years together.

Dr. Ma, typically, would finish eating before getting into the particulars of the crime she, *witnessed*. Always the consummate physician, she felt eating should be done in a calm mental state, sitting and of course, not talking.

David finished his meal rapidly and efficiently. Despite the speed of his consumption, he never suffered from digestive issues. He ate a mostly raw, plant based diet. Oddly enough for his animal spirit origin, a tiger, he did not consume meat.

He did put away a whopping amount of food in general. Always eating something, he had nuts, seeds, bars, protein powders and more in the small clinic fridge to keep him sustained throughout the day.

Dr. Ma put down her napkin and set aside the takeout container before beginning. She was very deliberate in her speech pattern, almost monotone at times. The effect could be quite hypnotic.

Her low, even tone, began the story of the Spirit Wind event.

Ma did not mention the Wind itself. She and David had never shared the complete circumstances of how she and he came about the information on the crime victims. Not with the police. Not even with Winnie.

Both Detective Brenner and Winnie knew that Dr. Ma and David were different. They accepted that Dr. Ma knew things in some psychic manner. After all, psychics were accepted today. For $3.99 a minute you could ask one anything you wanted to know about your life and your future.

Dr. Ma felt they considered her odd enough without adding her complete awareness of her current and past lives, her Elemental origins, even worse, the spiritual visitations of crime victims after they had passed.

She was very fond of Detective Brenner, and had to give him credit for dealing with her in the accepting manner that he did.

"I can draw the murder victim from memory for a sketch artist, Jeremy" she said. "I am sure she was a local club cyclist and that she was married. There should be a missing person bulletin out for her and the local A1A groups from Boca Raton to Ft. Lauderdale will know if a member is missing from the rides."

"We will start there to ID her, Dr. Ma. What condition is her face, her teeth, fingers and so forth in the event we fall short?" Detective Brenner asked, cutting right to the chase.

"Not good," Ma said shaking her head in the negative. "At this point, even worse I'm sorry to say. Poor thing. She was very pretty, once." Dr. Ma closed her eyes briefly to better reveal the scene in her memory. The less distractions from the outside, the greater the detail on the inside. This was a meditation technique that she and David emphasized to students over and over.

She pulled a notebook from her lab coat pocket and added a few lines to the sheet she had prepared. Ma handed the detective a written list of facts as she remembered them for his investigation. "As always Jeremy, these are the details as I saw them. Feel free to ask me any questions."

"Short curly blond hair, hazel eyes, about 5'2" and 100-110 pounds, physically fit. Wearing a matching cycling jersey and cycling shorts. Blue, black and white in color, but no visible Club name?" Brenner inquired.

"Could be the Coastal Triathlon Club," Ma answered. "She fell backwards when he hit her. The Club name should be on the back of the jersey and I never saw her back."

"Cervelo S5 Aero road bike, silver and yellow frame with black spoke wheels, handlebars and seat post," Brenner added, reading Dr. Ma's list.

"Distinctive," David said. That was an expensive bike from the description. David wasn't a cyclist like Dr. Ma but he dealt with quite a few pro's in clinical practice.

"Yes," Ma agreed. "The killer took it with him."

"I will check the local bike shops," Brenner said, furiously scribbling away on his old fashioned note pad.

"They wouldn't have bought it from him," Dr. Ma said. "He was dressed like a vagrant. They may have turned him away and or asked where he got it. They would know it was the prized possession of another cyclist."

"I doubt that he sold it to a legit Pawn Shop," Brenner frowned. "I'll check the back rooms of the other kind of shops."

Dr. Ma nodded grimly. "We will need a small motorized skiff to get to her." She is on a tiny round islet south of Bingham Island proper. If you start about the level of Bunker Road and Flagler and draw a straight line to Palm Beach Island it is the one by itself north of that line."

Detective Brenner startled, looked up, his face a comical expression of surprise. "Seriously?"

"Yes," Ma said. "He killed her in the parking area just past the bridge on the south side. She had stopped her bike there for whatever reason. "He dragged her…" She paused at this missing detail and decided to fill it in for now. "…Onto the island from there. I am surprised nobody saw this happen."

Brenner covered up his surprise in learning an actual murder occurred in his jurisdiction. Relatively, speaking. They would have to collaborate with the Palm Beach County Sheriff's Office, for sure. From there all sorts of coordinating and collaborating would be necessary with the State since the island was a wildlife preserve.

"I'm surprised he could get her very far onto the island or, better yet, to another one from there." Brenner closed his eyes picturing the site Dr. Ma was describing from memory. "Your notes say late afternoon early evening two days ago, Sunday?" Brenner inquired.
"Yes," Ma confirmed. "She was riding alone and dusk had just fallen. She was equipped to ride in the dark with a headlamp on her helmet and lights on her bike."

"Your killer walked up to her with a small cart of some type," Ma continued. "He had his hand out like he was asking for something. Money maybe?" Ma closed her eyes as she tried to re- call every detail. "She was standing with her back to the water facing north, the bike be- tween her and him. I think she knew something was off." Ma opened her eyes, looking at David briefly in confirmation.

"That was what I saw, too," David agreed.

Detective Brenner snapped his head around to look at David in surprise. This was the first time he had heard David clearly agree with a scene description. Good detective that he was, he said nothing. Let everyone else talk. Once the detective opened their mouths, the game changed.

David didn't actually have Dr. Ma's ability to see the scene in full detail. He couldn't hear and smell every nuance of the crime and environment. When he was with her, anchoring her so she could let herself go into the vision the Wind brought her, he could piggyback on some of her awareness.

Usually David would be able to see the landscape, the actors in the vision, basic movements and the rare sound, or smell. Sight wasn't his skill until recently. Dragons had second site. Dr. Ma also seem to have third, fourth, fifth and so on if you asked David's opinion.

Ma told him once that she could see every level of existence if she wished. She just had to focus. She didn't really *want* to see all those levels too often. Too much information was distracting. It was too fatiguing to sort through the influx of details.

David, being a tiger, couldn't see all the planes of existence. Tigers were typical cats. They could see easily on the first one to two planes of existence. David being an Elemental could get another level or so from just the essence of his being, but that was about it.

For David, seeing what Ma was seeing in a Wind event was like hopping a ride with her visually. Problem was, much of it got obscured by the elements of the psychic storm the Spirit Wind brought.

Dr. Ma was powerful in the Ether. Dragons were creatures of the air element. She could see things that could only be seen in the otherworldly dimensions. She could even pass through these dimensions in her Elemental form if necessary.

David was the master of skills on the ground in the human realm. Tigers belonged to the earth element. At the crime scene he would be the powerful eyes and ears that could ferret out details left behind in the current earthly dimension.

Detective Brenner cleared his throat to interrupt the brief silence. He was used to Dr. Ma and David wandering off mentally while describing a scene. He was pretty sure they were silently communicating with each other at times. When this occurred, he would bring them back on track with a polite interruption. "And then?" he said.

"The killer reached back to his cart as if he was getting something out for her," Dr. Ma continued. "The man started to turn back towards her and shifted his weight from the right foot to the left, bringing his right fist around and smashed it into her face."

Dr. Ma closed her eyes again. She let all the sounds, smells and feelings flood her consciousness. Not the best choice after a full meal. It would interrupt with a smooth and efficient digestion.

She was also vulnerable in this state of altered awareness. There was no immediate threat sitting in the clinic, but any voluntary movement would be delayed, several seconds or more in the event she had to respond. If David wasn't sitting next to her she would not risk this step back in memory unprotected. He would defend her if anything *unexpected* occurred. It had happened before.

Dr. Ma felt and heard things in her memory of the event. It was as if it was occurring in that moment.

Crack! The woman's facial bones snapped with the force of the blow. The vagrant had chapped and dirty skin on his hands and forearms. His closed fist was calloused on the knuckles. From fighting for survival, probably.
The woman's upper jaw, the maxilla, had cracked slightly, but not the lower jaw. That wasn't broken yet. Dr. Ma felt the force of the impact, ricochet her brain and torque the cervical spine so significantly that the woman went limp immediately.

"Good shot," Ma thought, "you must be a helluva fighter in the vagrant world." That, or an ex-boxer with that form.

You never know who will end up on the street.

After the blow, from the killer's fist to her face, the woman tumbled to the ground, like an unwanted rag doll, dropped suddenly from a child's arms, who had lost interest in playing with her. Too bad the killer's interest was just beginning.

Her bicycle fell on top of her as she collapsed, causing small injuries that would be consistent with the frame of the bike impacting soft tissue. Dr. Ma made mental note to share this with Detective Brenner. The murder victim would have a gouge on her left shin from the pedal and a broken right thumb from her fall.

It was so unexpected, that blow to the face, that the woman hadn't even tried to shield herself. Dr. Ma remembered the underlying anger and surprise she felt from the Spirit of the now deceased woman. That is the problem with the normal person. They don't expect violent behavior. You have to train this expectation into people. That is what they do in the military, law enforcement and of course in neighborhoods rife with crime.

Dr. Ma described all this in detail to Detective Brenner.

"It happened very fast, Jeremy," she said. "He pulled her bike off her and quickly dragged her to that opening onto Bingham Island where the chain link fence is bent back. The size of the opening gives animals access to the island itself, but it is so overgrown at the tree line a human cannot really pass."

Murder Scene

West Palm
Beach

Flagler Drive

Southern Boulevard Causeway

⊗

Jack
hits
Karen

Bingham
Island

Karen
found
dead

N
W ⟷ E
S

"How did he get her down the island and onto the islet where you say she is?" Brenner asked.

"That is where it gets obscured," Dr. Ma replied. She wasn't ready to discuss this until she and David did some onsite investigation, later. She needed to confirm the involvement she felt from the otherworldly being. The smell. "I will let you know more as it comes to me."

Brenner looked up in surprise. "What did you say?" He had never heard her say something was obscured in a vision.

Ma frowned and looked at David. David also wore a strangely serious expression.

Looking at them both, Brenner felt a moment of confusion. He had never seen David not at least partly smiling. The man was always happy and peaceful. It didn't seem natural.

Deciding to be as honest as possible, Dr. Ma replied "David and I will have to go there to answer that, Jeremy. I sense the killer and his victim moving along the west side of Bingham Island and ending up on that little islet, but I do not see clearly *how* it was done. That concerns me."

"Me too," Brenner said, meaning it. He had known Dr. Ma long enough to expect the unexpected. Of course it would just make things more difficult to explain from a police perspective.

"Go to one of your residents' homes that has a backyard capable of overlooking that islet to the west," Dr. Ma advised Detective Brenner. "Take binoculars and see if you can see anything. Tell someone you had a tip from a passing boater."

"What if I can't see anything?" Brenner asked. This was a reflexive question he would ask a normal person. Why it came out of his mouth while speaking to Dr. Ma, he didn't know. If she had told him to look, he would see what he needed to. It never failed.

"You will," Ma replied smiling. She knew he regretted the question almost immediately after asking it. "Check a couple backyard views but don't give up. I know you need a direct chain of evidence for your investigation, but you will get it."
"Ok then. Thanks for lunch," Brenner said, standing up quickly and stuffing his notepad with her list into his pocket. "I'll call you as soon as I have something."

"Thank you, Jeremy," Ma replied. "When your crime scene investigation is done, David and I will visit the location with you. Nothing they do will interfere with our ability to help you investigate."

"I know," Brenner grinned at her. "I'm counting on it."

Detective Brenner unlocked the front door to leave and Winnie locked it again right behind him. She knew Dr. Ma and David had more to say in Brenner's absence. She would make herself scarce. Her input wasn't necessary for that discussion.

"I'm going to the kitchen to clean up," Winnie announced. She scooped up all the empty takeout containers and left. "I'm heading to the bank and the Post Office afterward," she called over her shoulder as she headed down the hall.

Dr. Ma valued her assistant's discretion. She knew Winnie was bursting with questions and curiosity about the murder. She would include her after they had more information. Right now, there was too much she couldn't share with the older woman.

Ma turned to David. "Good to go there later tonight?" she asked.

"Of course," David responded with a broad smile. He was excited to take action themselves on this situation. The fact that Ma couldn't see what happened during a portion of the vision meant something other than mundane human events had occurred.

"The usual time on the west side of the bridge?" Ma asked. She would need room to get up speed and a clean field to do it on. There wasn't much traffic there at 3:00 AM.

"You and I have that social event tonight. Barring anything unusual, you'll be home by nine or ten, and I should be clear by midnight," David replied. David frequently stayed later than Dr. Ma at these events.

"Sounds good," Dr. Ma replied, carefully eyeing David. "Be careful after I leave you tonight." She knew there would be the inevitable invitations for the stunning young man. He had a harder time dealing with human attraction than she did. She enjoyed herself, but always went home alone.

David James Anderson III was how he had returned in this lifetime. The orphaned son of wealthy European and Middle Eastern parentage, he had more money than anyone with his lifestyle would need. The orphan thing seemed to be a recurring theme in his re-manifestations.

Dr. Ma also found her way back in a family that would soon leave her solo. She re-manifested differently that David. He had to be reborn. In Ma's case she would step into a life that was held as a place marker for her. Neither could have close, living relatives for long. It was necessary for their work to minimize ties to the human world around them.

When David was ready, Ma would always find him, and adopt him. Allistair and his crew kept tabs on David with the help of their immortal astrologer, Donald Lake. He could pinpoint anything they needed in time on one of his fancy charts. Even Dr. Ma was amazed at his accuracy.

David was the only thing Dr. Ma needed tracked with careful precision. He was more vulnerable in human form than she was. His early demise would mean a significant delay in doing their job. She hadn't worked without him for almost a thousand years, since her mate moved on.

Dr. Ma was about eighteen to twenty years his senior each time they came together again. Since she stepped into the life of a place marker, there wasn't that much a difference in time. Only a few years may separate their reunion in the human realm.

For David, what Dr. Ma did in the interim before he came back he never really knew or cared. He knew she waited to do what they did until they were together again. That was the way it had been arranged by the creators.

David knew he would spend the first eight to ten years of his life without her. It gave both of them time to assimilate into the currents of human existence as they were at the time. You had to be careful about mistakes in front of humans. The illusion needed careful tending.

Neither Dr. Ma nor David worried about what happened to the other during their brief time of separation. There was always a type of awareness that the other was on this plane of existence when they were apart. David knew the Astrologer kept track of his comings and goings.

It really didn't matter. They had their jobs to do. They would meet up somewhere. Then they would pass this next time around, together.

The rest of the day went by quickly with the usual complaints from their patients. They both loved the work they were doing in this lifetime.

Winnie came back from lunch and her errands just as the last patient was leaving. It had taken longer than expected at the Post Office and bank. Dr. Ma and David took over her duties as much as possible when she wasn't in the office. Thank goodness for that computer-based program that Dr. Ma had installed last year. Patients could check in and out and even pay with a card Winnie made for them. They just had to interact with a large computer monitor on the front desk.

Neither Winnie nor Dr. Ma preferred this impersonal approach. It was only used as needed. Winnie usually reached out, and took the patient's card for them and did the transaction. She would rather they be sitting comfortably on the couch with a hot tea.

Dr. Ma set out the muffins she baked this morning for Winnie's birthday and a small wrapped box. Winnie was delighted by the baked goods but even more so by the small signature blue box from Tiffany. The doctors were always generous with her gifts. Inside the tiny box was nestled a pair of gold Paloma Picasso Olive Leaf, drop earrings.

Dr. Ma had incredible taste. Winnie held back tears as she thanked them both. "They are just beautiful, thank you both so much." At this rate, Winnie thought, her daughter was going to have quite an inheritance. Winnie and Bud had gone through serious financial woes when Bud was diagnosed with cancer.

When Dr. Ma had hired her as her personal assistant and clinic manager, some top tier medical benefits and a major salary increase had turned everything around. Winnie and Bud would never be able to express how much Dr. Ma and David had done to change their lives for the better.

Both Ma and David sang 'Happy Birthday' to her. Each had a muffin and then David had one more. Winnie snatched the plate away as he reached for the third muffin.

I'll take the rest home," Winnie said, giving David her most formidable look.

"No worries, Winnie," David said. He pointed at Dr. Ma. "We are going to a charity event tonight. There will be plenty of food there."

"I hope," he thought, as he remembered the offerings from the last few events he had been to. It had seemed like a long line of sweets and high fat foods.

David knew that the ladies attending did not keep their ultra slim bodies by eating that type food at these events. Dr. Ma didn't eat much of the offered fare either. Neither of them had any reason to count calories. It was simply a matter of only consuming food that was a benefit to your body and its function. Just when you think people were turning more and more to healthy fare, they surprised you and went crazy with party food.

Today David made an exception in his mostly raw diet for Dr. Ma's delicious muffins. Tonight was a *South African Save the Tigers* event. He hoped there would be an offering of fruits, vegetables and nuts. That, would fall solidly into his preferred eating range.

David made a face at Dr. Ma. "Right? Plenty of food?"

"I will pick you up at 6:30 sharp," Dr. Ma said laughing. "Lets grab a quick bite at Renato's before we go, so you won't starve. I mean it's an event for tigers, that can't be your kind of diet."

"Ha ha," he replied silently. "You're killing me." Aloud, he said, "Great idea!"
Dr. Ma smiled and headed to her office to pick up her car keys and briefcase. "Would you like a ride home to save a little time?" David usually ran to work before his early class.
David nodded and followed her. "Goodnight Winnie, see you tomorrow."

Winnie noted the silent part of David's exchange and wondered. There was always something they weren't telling her. "Goodnight! Enjoy your charity thing. Patients are starting at 9 AM sharp. Thank you again for the earrings and muffins." Dr. Ma smiled back at her. The two of them were never late.

Arriving at his Palm Beach digs, David thanked Dr. Ma for the ride. "I'll see you soon," he said over his shoulder, hurrying up his stairs. "Save the tigers," he thought. "A bit ironic wasn't it?" He would definitely write the organization a big check. There would be an outpouring of bad jokes from their attorney, when he saw the donation amount.

Allistair oversaw every expenditure David and Dr. Ma made from their personal accounts. The attorney missed nothing.

Davis's apartment was quiet, cool and always slightly damp from the old stones that made up the 100 year old walls. David walked to the south side window overlooking the restaurant's courtyard seating. The smell of pasta and bread drifted up from the courtyard of the restaurant below his apartment windows.

David would fill up on raw or partly steamed veggies. He made a quick call to the restaurant to tell them he and Dr. Ma would be eating there in about an hour. It was season and no reservations were available in general, but the maitre d' always had a place for them.

David could manage to eat at most places on the island, but he liked the legendary Italian eatery conveniently located next to his apartment. It would be delicious and satisfying. David knew tonight's late visit to the crime scene with Dr. Ma would burn some serious calories.

Dr. Ma made the 5-minute trip home from David's apartment to her residence, quickly showered and dressed, in a stunning St. John white silk sheath printed with abstract black flowers. Chic but conservative. Ma's long inky black hair fell straight to her waist, parted in the middle. The thick hair was like a shimmering accessory.

She checked her look in the long mirror of her dressing room and added an elegant pair of black pearl earrings. An onyx cuff adorned one wrist. Her other hand held a small glittering black clutch. Sky high, red silk, Louboutin heels finished the image looking back at her from the mirror.

She glanced briefly at the Intracoastal Waterway through the wall of frameless glass. The entire east side of her home on Flagler Drive was glass. She looked in the direction of the murder scene. She silently promised the victim to catch her killer. Dr. Ma was back at David's apartment in under an hour.

David was waiting on the sidewalk when she pulled up. He quickly paid for her parking with his cellphone. Reaching to help her out of her Mercedes C63 AMG Coupe, his eyes took her in appreciatively. "How can you be so beautiful at your age?" he teased. "By the way, I really love that car."

Dr. Ma had picked Mars Red for the color when she order the coupe. "I would give it to you if I could trust you to drive," she teased. "And what do you mean exactly by my age?"

David bent and kissed her cheek. Elegantly attired in a custom navy Italian wool suit, his tanned skin contrasted perfectly with the ivory silk crew neck shirt underneath the jacket. "He smells earthly, masculine," she thought. No wonder he has such problems!

"Keep it up young man, and I will show you how old I am," Dr. Ma said wiggling her eyebrows. In an old fashioned gesture, David gently took her hand and placed it on his arm to escort her into the restaurant. His body shivered. They went to enjoy a quick dinner before the charity event.

Chapter Six - Midnight On The Lagoon

Time to go. Dr. Ma's eyes snapped open. The projection clock on the ceiling read 3:30 AM. She was fully dressed in the same black training gear as earlier in the day, at the dojo. Her fashionable evening clothes had been neatly put away, when she arrived home from the charity tiger event.

She enjoyed attending these events. Benefiting the charity was first. Second was the entertainment of the invited guests.

This evening they had been at a private home on Wells Road. Charity events on the Island were mostly about social interaction, drinking and at times, debauchery. Any event was just an excuse for a party. In a town that thrived on parties for every possible reason, it was the acceptable way to raise money.

There was always intrigue, who was seen with whom. Who wasn't see with whom? Who left with, before or after whom? And, of course, the most important of all, how were the guests, mostly the ladies, attired?

Dr. Ma had fabulous fashion sense. Her outfits were always chosen to compliment her. Not the other way around. There was a lot of the clothing wearing the person, going on at these events. She attracted more than her share of attention from how she looked.

Then there was David. Always meticulously dressed in tailored suits or separates, he was the center of attention for the younger female crowd, the older female crowd, and the younger and older gay male crowd. Dr. Ma enjoyed watching him negotiate them all night.

The large showing of people wanting to be entertained at least benefitted the main cause. A tiger reserve in South Africa. Poaching the big cats was out of control. Where the desire for tiger penis in Chinese Medicine had come from, Dr. Ma did not know. She had been around for millennia and that was never a viable remedy for impotence.

Arriving back home at about 10:00 PM, she changed quickly and laid down to rest until it was time to go. David had stayed later at the event as usual. Several women had been dogging his every step, when she last saw him. She wished him all the best, but she would prefer he got some downtime to be at his best for the investigation. Something kept nagging at her about the murder. She was looking forward to seeing it tonight with sharper eyes. Dragon's eyes. Add David's incredible night vision and there would be nothing missed.

Dr. Ma rested but didn't actually sleep. Her consciousness was always awake. A few hours of delta state meditation would work wonders.

Ma didn't dream. A delta state produced no REM. She didn't have a typically human brain, despite her current human manifestation. Deepening her brain waves was her way of giving her central nervous system a full break from activity.

Elementals were able to move freely between brain wave states. Beta, Alpha, Theta and Delta were common human brain wave cycles. Gamma was less frequent with humans but more a normal state for Elementals.

She closed the front door behind her, briefly touching the invisible seal on the outside. Human burglars wouldn't notice, but they would pick another location to rob for some reason they wouldn't be able to explain.

The reason behind this layer of otherworldly security had less to do with human intrusion than otherworldly invasion. Dr. Ma wanted a secure location to return and recharge. She had no fear of most otherworldly beings. She just didn't want to be bothered dealing with them anytime they wandered by.

The sky was a dark blue velvet color with tiny sparkles of light attached to its fabric. The moon was full without any cloud covering. It always seemed like the moonlight laid a silver carpet along the Intracoastal waterway for you to follow on its best and brightest evening showings.

She checked her shoelaces and took off with purpose. No relaxed run tonight, she had work to do. She and David were keeping a tight time schedule. Start when most humans were deeply asleep and home from evening social activities. Finish before even the early birds had risen. Less chance of being seen.

Running quickly, she retraced her northerly route from that morning. The evening provided a damp chilliness, common in South Florida this time of year. Being next to the water allowed a soft fog to obscure the path and bathe the streetlights in gauzy curtains.

Jamil was awake when she passed. Sensing her intent, he roused himself further away from his typical tree sleep. Ma knew he could pull his spiritual essence from the tree without harming it. If she needed him that was. If for some reason it all went south. She didn't foresee such a need, but it was comforting knowing he was ready.

"I will watch for you, Ma-sama," Jamil called. "Count on my help if you need it."

"You are a true friend, Great One," Dr. Ma replied over her shoulder as she raced past him.

Soft chattering voices came from the water of the Intracoastal. She recognized them as water Sprites. Their tinny voices were difficult to understand when they all spoke at once. She got the impression they were also lending their assistance tonight if needed.

"Thank you friends," she said in general towards the area their voices came from. She heard soft splashes as they disappeared below the water's surface, for now. They were little more than smudges against the choppy water. The moonlight only increased the glare on the water to hide their passage.

At night or in complete darkness, the pupils of Dr. Ma's lapis blue eyes glowed yellow gold. This is how she saw clearly without any light source. Her vision was as good as in the full brightness of a South Florida day.

David had such eyes. In the dark, David's vision was much better than it was in daylight. His night vision was superior to hers unless she used her dragon senses.

She could see David's glowing eyes looking south, waiting for her. "On time, I see," Dr. Ma thought. David heard her and smiled in response, his teeth flashing white, briefly. The foliage near the intersection of Flagler Drive and Southern Boulevard shrouded the corner where he stood. Dressed in black like her, little was visible.

He turned away and started running as she approached. The two of them became a blur of motion as they sprinted east over the Southern Boulevard bridge towards Bingham Island and the recent murder scene.

Leaping into the air just past the apex of the bridge Ma stretched her arms and felt them transform. Long elegant black wings covered a

15 foot span as she rose silently into the night air.

Her black training gear seamlessly transformed into the tight black skin of the dragon she became. The inky mass of hair that normally flowed down her back became the scales of her beast. She hadn't remembered to pull it into a braid after the event. Powerful wings beating the air, she rose up and up, her muscular legs now tucking under her in flight.

Dr. Ma always wondered about those fictional beings that shape-shifted in books and movies so popular today. They were always ripping to shreds or removing, their clothing. Why did they not transform their clothing as easily as she and David? Didn't anyone pay attention in physics class? Matter changes into other forms. David was half her age and he could transform seamlessly into his beast.

Ma tilted her head as she swept down to hover over the crime scene. Her sharp predator eyes pierced the darkness. In dragon form, her vision was incredibly sharp. So was her hearing and sense of smell. Noting the large variety of living creatures on the little island she refined her search mentally for human and non animal traces.

David had transformed, too. A massive tiger paced below her sniffing the ground, delicately avoiding the crime scene tape that the police department had left to shroud the location. He lifted his massive head and bared his teeth at her. Not aggressive, just the tiger version of his ever present grin. This one was more visible than before in human guise, due to the sheer volume of enamel on the monstrous canines and incisors.

His powerful body was almost obscured in the dark. He had a very unusual coat coloration.

David transformed into the rarest of genetic presentations in tigers. Deep steel gray with black stripes, he would give the heart of Jack Hanna from Busch Gardens a pause. His eyes remained their deep blue with yellow gold pupil rings, just like Ma's.

They looked at each other in silent understanding. Let's get this thing done. Every minute they remained transformed, was a risk of discovery by humans. The tree spirits around them gathered a bit more fog to drape their branches in. The water Sprites gathered closer to the island and its islet strand and pushed more in between the trees. "Thank you," both Dr. Ma and David sent out mentally.

While Ma swept silently over the tree tops looking down for clues, David waded into the Intracoastal waterway to swim the perimeter of the marshy overgrown island.

A little known fact about tigers, they were strong swimmers. Tigers could even kill prey in the water and drag it to shore to eat. David would have no problem negotiating the deep water side of the island, or anything swimming around in it. Not the Sprites of course, they were being helpful tonight.

The island's population of hawks and birds of prey were oddly still as Dr. Ma passed over in her Elemental dragon form. Their deepest instincts told them that a much more dangerous predator than they were, was flying overhead. This fearful knowledge passed to every living creature on and around the island as Dr. Ma and David searched for clues.

The night's stillness became crystal clear with the two Elementals hunting around it. It seemed that nothing would dare to breathe until they were done. Not that they would harm any creature living on the small island and it's surrounding areas.

The energetic signature where the human killer passed from the south side of the Southern Boulevard Causeway through the island was very strange. The line went straight from where he had first encountered her by the roadway, at the east end of the bridge, south, to the islet where her body was found.

It passed through a heavily wooded, thick underbrush covering the island. Some spaces so tight only things that could fly or crawl would go. There was no path, no space sufficient, to allow a full size human passage. Let alone a full size human carrying or dragging another full sized human.
"Impossible!" Dr Ma thought.

She carefully inspected the east side of the island for any traces. None were there. She knew David was carefully inspecting the west side of the island.

"Anything?" she asked silently.

"Absolutely nothing," he replied.

"What was weirder still," Ma thought, was that the signature line of the killers passage was interspersed with another fine line. It was a second signature! But it wasn't human. What was moving along with the killer through an impass-able overgrown island?" All the while, carrying a woman's unconscious or dying body.

Dr. Ma and David finally met up on the tiny round islet where the murdered woman had so recently been found. Her body lay there until Detective Brenner arrived, awaiting discovery. Ma folded her wings and landed lightly as David pulled himself up on to an outcropping of tree roots.

The massive tiger shook off the dirty water of the Intracoastal, spraying Dr. Ma and the tiny islet with droplets. The base of the islet consist-ed mainly of tree roots and the debris they had trapped to grow into.

Dr. Ma gave him a dark look as the oily liquid landed on her black skin. The waterway was filthy with the by-products of boating. Dr. Ma remembered a triathlon competition last year in that very waterway. When the swimmers re-moved their goggles coming out of the water, the pollution was obvious. White rings showed around their eyes, contrasting with their then darker than normal faces.

The tiger opened its mouth fully, tongue lolling. "Not funny," Ma communicated to him silently.

"Get out of that wet fur before you start to smell. We are done here for now."

David quickly transformed to his human shape. The grin was still present from his success of getting her wet. "You know you look like that pet dragon from the kids' movie I just saw with our white belts," David said.

Dr. Ma actually didn't look much different in transformation. Not like David. She stood about two feet taller. She was definitely heavier. But other than the black skin, scales and wings, she appeared pretty much the same.

She bared her teeth at him, this time. "You are really pushing your luck boy," she said. Most of it came out as a barely intelligible hiss, but he could understand her perfectly after all their time together. In her dragon form, Ma's speech was only clearly understood in pure thoughts.

"Ready?" Ma sent at him.

"Whenever you are," David replied somewhat less enthusiastically.

Extending her wings and lifting up a few feet, Ma bent down to wrap her arms around David's waist for the brief flight to shore. A few powerful beats of her wings, and they were climbing.

Continuing upward, Ma felt David squirming. Tigers weren't fans of heights, but she was going to get a little pay back for the shower of dirty water she just experienced.

Soaring to about three hundred feet, she suddenly nosed dived. David went stiff in her arms, she knew his eyes were closed, stomach dropping.

She pulled up less than a foot from landing on the sidewalk next to Flagler Drive, and dropped him none too gently.

To David's credit he landed on his feet and stayed there. "Graceful cat!" she thought.

"Humorless dragon!" David sent her way. Laughter from the water Sprites echoed around them. David turned towards the little creatures, growling low in his throat. Several splashes announced their rapid departure.

Ma landed next to him, fully transforming as she did.

"Well, we know he wasn't alone in this," Ma said. She was referring to the slender thread of energy, another signature besides the killer. It was woven in and around every inch of the signature the actual killer left behind. This was not what they had been looking for. It was a surprise to say the least. They would know more in human form. Some senses were shut down when they transformed.

"Definitely not," David agreed. He bent down, re-tying his running shoes before his trip home.

"We can get more on the island tomorrow in daylight," Ma said. "The island itself will give us more information. By the way, how long did you stay at the event last night?"

David shook his head as an answer. He didn't look particularly happy. "Must not have worked out with any of his numerous admirers," Dr. Ma thought. "I think it is a worthwhile donation for us after talking to the organizers," she said aloud.

"Yes, I agree," David said still looking away, still seeming to be uncomfortable.

Ma knew not to pry. He would tell her in good time. "Alright then, see you in the morning?"

"I'll be in class as usual when you get there" David said. Turning to go, he stopped when he heard Jamil's voice.

"Are you done for the night?" Jamil's voice carried through the darkness. Humans would have only heard a sharp rustling of limbs clacking against each other.

"Yes, old man," David replied loudly enough to carry back. Everyone knew trees were slightly hard of hearing. "I didn't know you woke Jamil to help us," he said more softly to Dr. Ma.

"I didn't," Ma replied. "He seems very awake lately, something is up."

David paused another moment and looked at her. "That energy signature is bothering me."

"Agreed," Dr. Ma said with a sigh.

"So did you get a read on who else was involved?" David asked her. Dr. Ma was the master of the ethereal. Tonight, any clues from the Ether was what they were looking for.

"Not exactly," she replied. I have an identifiable signature. I will know him when I come in contact with him."

"So male killer and male collaborator?" David confirmed. He was proud of himself for getting a clear read on the sex of the perpetrators. Male and female human scents were sharply defined for a big cat.

"Yes," Ma said. "One didn't know her, the killer, but I get the distinct feeling that the other one did."

David nodded, and they both turned away this time for their respective homes. Dr. Ma was running again in a few feet. She faintly heard David's footfalls increase as he started running as well. She was less than a mile from home now. David had to cross the bridge again and run north along the island to his apartment off Worth Avenue.

Tomorrow would bring more information. Tonight they made the discovery that the killer hadn't acted alone. He was manipulated by someone else. Someone with a strong other-worldly energetic signature. Someone that Dr. Ma and David would be uniquely capable of finding.

Chapter Seven - The Doctors Take A Field Trip

Dr. Ma and David were both on time the next morning. Winnie ran a tight ship, no matter how late they were out investigating.

"Winnie?" Ma called to her faithful friend and assistant. "A minute?"

Winnie materialized in Ma's doorway, her usual frowning countenance simply misunderstood, for the genial smile it hid beyond most people's recognition.

Ma had known Winnie for years. However, Ma's ability to see human beings as they actually were, gave no pause to her with Winnie's expression. In fact, to her, it appeared Winnie *was* smiling.

Today Dr. Ma had to leave early to meet with Detective Brenner. They were arranging an unofficial visit to the location where the body of the murdered young woman from her vision was killed, and the second site where the body was left to rot. If Ma hadn't told Detective Brenner where to find it, that is.

.

David would be going with her, so some patient appointments had to be rearranged. She needed the tiger to help her gather important physical clues left behind. The ones not seen by the human investigators.

"How difficult will it be to open up the afternoon Winnie? Say after 2:00 PM?" Ma asked her. They walked out front to Winnie's desk.

"Not a problem, Dr. Ma," Winnie replied, checking the large paper schedule. Dr. Ma sighed to herself as she saw the big paper pad on the desk. No matter what type of high end computer based practice software they used, Winnie had to have a paper fall back.

"Dr. David has two performance assessments that the new strength training coach can handle. Your afternoon nutrition group can use the time to catch up on reading and prepping the two dishes themselves. I'll help them of course." Winnie said all of this in her efficient and clipped tone.
Dr. Ma smiled. Winnie was a good cook and loved to help with the nutrition group when she could. Never a healthy eater, Winnie had to learn differently when her husband Bud had been diagnosed with cancer. Now with Ma's

help, Winnie was becoming quite the healthy food chef.

"How is Gina doing?" Ma asked, inquiring about the new strength coach.

"Pretty good so far," Winnie responded. Dr. Ma watched carefully for any signs of sarcasm, but saw none. Well then, that was big praise from Winnie! Dr. Ma and David hired Gina a few months ago to handle the strength training recovery work for their competitive athletes. Not all their athletes. Just the ones who weren't already so high on the food chain that they had their own coaches who came with them.

Adding personalized recovery training had become too much for the two busy doctors and they were glad to have Gina recommended by one of their pro athlete's coaches. The coach had worked with her in the past, and had nothing but good things to say about her.

Gina was short for Angelina. A former Olympic gymnast, Angelina Debecker was now, Gina Stiller. She married Sam Stiller, a local accountant, and settled in the area last year. It didn't take long for her to get bored and start scouting for a job. Dr. Ma hired her after her first interview.

"How is Detective Brenner doing so far?" Winnie inquired. She tried to contain her excitement over the murder investigation. She wasn't forgetting someone died. She just loved all the intrigue about finding the killer.

"He was able to see what appeared to be a body, on the islet, from a backyard with binoculars, as we hoped. They recovered her body yesterday and are still going over the crime scene today," Ma answered. "Detective Brenner will be able to get us onto the site this afternoon."

Dr. Ma and Detective Brenner had first, met when he was shot on the job, a couple years ago.

Palm Beach Police Department simply did not have officer shootings. The quiet island was not a high crime location. Well, not since April 30th,1951, when Hugh Berry shot officer Tyler Watts in a psychotic break. Watts survived, as did Hugh's father Thomas, who was also shot. Hugh's 80 year old grandmother Ella McClung, died a week later of her injuries.
Shooting an officer was big news on the island of Palm Beach and likely to make Brenner a folk hero for years to come, even after retirement. Brenner had started out in Miami Metro

PD as a rookie and never looked back after his move to Palm Beach.

The fact that he was shot, doing his job on the famous island versus Metro-Dade, was irony not lost on the dedicated young man. Ma had told him that you can never escape your fate, it just changes locations with you. Every time he saw the scar from the bullet in the mirror, he believed her.

Being assigned as a homicide detective on an island that had seen 5 murders in 100 years of its history could be a bit slow. Until now. Number six. It wouldn't go over well at the next Town Council meeting.

Detective Brenner took Dr. Ma's Tai Chi class, after being shot, to rehabilitate. Both doctors worked steadily to repair both Brenner's physical strength and mental clarity. Brenner thought he was better after the shooting than before.

Today, Brenner *was* stronger mentally and physically than before he was shot, due mostly to their influence on him. After all, once your fears have been realized, and you survive, things that loomed large often fall back into the smaller perspective that they deserved in the first place.

"Do you think her killer is likely to target some-one else?" Winnie asked, gently prying for more details.

"No, Winnie," Dr. Ma smiled grimly. "He meant to just kill her. I don't think another murder is in his future. Besides, Detective Brenner will have him in custody very soon."

"Oh good," Winnie said, somewhat reluctantly backing out of the office. "Wouldn't want a seri-al killer on the loose." She would love to hear more details. Unfortunately for Winnie, the front door chime was announcing patient arrivals.

Dr. Ma smiled again as Winnie closed her office door. Never wish for something that is going to happen anyway, Winnie. A serial criminal was always right around the corner, just awaiting their opportunity. Her office door opened again to reveal David's smiling face.

"Winnie prospecting for details?" David asked feigning innocence.

"Of course!" Ma replied laughing. "That woman is on a need to know, as in 'I always need to know,' basis. That is one of the things that makes her a great assistant and office manag-er."

"Especially for this office," she thought, without saying it aloud.

"Are we good to go for this afternoon?" he asked.

"Yes," Ma replied. "Your training evals are in Gina's capable hands, and my nutrition class will be in Winnie's."

"Winnie will be taking over your class soon," David smiled with real affection. He genuinely cared for the older woman, no matter how often she grumbled at him.

"Exactly what I hope for," Ma replied. "David?" Ma said questioningly.
"Yes," David responded slowly, reaching for the thoughts behind Ma's words. He came up empty. Her mind was closed to him at the moment, so she could structure her words ,without revealing her exact thoughts. He really disliked being shut out.

"Gina is a lovely young lady," Ma said carefully.

"She is a *married,* lovely young lady," David came back quickly.

"She is a lovely young lady with a pulse, and her husband is older. They haven't much in common, I have come to understand. You *are* extending your no involvement clause with your students, patients, clients, and co-workers to include her? Right?,"

"Ma!" David put on his best shocked expression. "That is taboo. Not exactly because she is married but she is definitely a co-worker."

"Good to hear," Ma replied with quiet sarcasm.

"No, really," David said, dropping his bantering tone. "She was flirting the other day while we were working, and I had 'the talk' with her." "I'm sorry, David," Ma said, feeling sympathy for the handsome but rather lonely young man. "I know you struggle with all the attention and flirting. I am still working on an amulet or some other object you can wear. Maybe we can mask that rather extreme attraction level your manifestation laid on you this time around. It must be tiring."

They were speaking very openly now, no sarcasm, no joking. Dr. Ma adopted David when he was 10 years old. She had been shocked at the sexual magnetism he already exuded so young. It seemed to get stronger each time.

She thought it was because the tiger had never found a mate in all his years. Partners yes, a mate, no.

She had been horrified at the physical abuse he had endured before she located him this time. A powerful tiger he could take a great deal of pain and suffering physically. Mentally, he was the gentle underbelly of the beast. He always had been. Ma felt compelled to do something to help him, but a solution had so far escaped her.

David, dealt with it well, she had to admit. Constant fawning attention and outright plays for him, were kept to a minimum with his somewhat solitary existence. When he attended charity or social events, however, things could get out of hand.

Strict rules of engagement at the clinic and dojo kept things in check there.

Dr. Ma did not suffer from the same issues as David. Her issues were more appropriate to the reflective and reticent nature of the dragon. She had a difficult time getting close to humans. They always had an underlying fear of her.

When she attended social events with David, for his protection mostly, she was beyond stunning. A gorgeous physical form, elegant legs, glittering hair to her waist and a killer figure brought many looks, but few offers. Dr. Ma was beautiful, but imposing, in some indescribable way.

They smiled at each other, allowing the quiet pause between them to expand and surround their thoughts. Old spirits, old friends, forever entwined.

Winnie poked her head around the half open office door.

"Are you planning on canceling the morning or are you two going to get going?"

"Yes ma'am," David replied giving Winnie a quick peck on the cheek as he passed.

Winnie blushed and slapped him gently as he left. "Yes," Ma thought, "even you, Winnie, are vulnerable to David's charms."

The morning went quickly. Ma had several patients she was in the middle of treatment plans for. The chiropractor with the torn rotator cuff. The financial advisor with the upper leg injury.

The young female tennis player with the low back pain. She was the same young tennis player who made eyes at David whenever she saw him in the hall or reception area of the clinic.

When the time finally came to go they grabbed a couple of David's snack bars for lunch and headed out to meet Detective Brenner.

He met them at the small parking area, east of the Southern Boulevard bridge, on the south side. Ma got out of the car and closed her eyes briefly. Memories of the Spirit Wind swept around her. Tendrils and whispers now, not the full onslaught.

She reached deeper to get a strong grip on the information she had absorbed. She could smell fear now, anger, and a sense of loss, as the victim realized her fate. She could hear the crunch, again, as the woman's facial bones broke under the impact of the killer's fist.

Ma could sense the fading of the victim's consciousness.

Then there was that strange nothingness, until the murder victim, partly woke up on the little islet. The final blow that ended her existence came there. The piece of concrete debris clutched tightly in the killer's hand was the final murder weapon. He held it so tightly his hand had been cut across the palm. There was so much blood. Most was hers but some of it was his.

"Jeremy, there will be some concrete chunk, with the killer's DNA. He cut himself on it, when he smashed her mouth and teeth in," Ma said

Brenner nodded, scribbling away on the ever present note pad. He took in the information with no outward sign of revulsion. They were just facts. Information needed to catch the killer. Emotion interfered with objectivity.

David made a low sound in his throat. She knew he was seeing some of what she was reviewing in her mind. "Was that a growl? Perhaps so," Dr. Ma thought. She knew the victim's suffering angered David as much as it did her.

"What was going on, in that unknown, in-between time, she couldn't see?" Dr. Ma mused. "What could obscure the path the killer had taken to move the body from here?"

Both David and Dr. Ma noted the increasing number of people arriving in the small parking lot on the north side across from where they stood.

"Logistics," Detective Brenner said, noting their interest.

"For?" Ma inquired.

"It is a bird Preserve, State guys making sure the wildlife isn't disturbed. County guys making sure the State guys aren't disturbed. Last but not least, my guys, making sure I am not disturbed."

"Well said," Ma grinned.

"Do you feel undisturbed?" David asked Detective Brenner, teasing gently.

"No, as a matter of fact, I am very disturbed," Brenner said seriously. "Lets get this killer."

Ma knew that Brenner had seen the young woman's face. What was left of it.

He had seen where, the piece of broken concrete, was jammed into her mouth, to fracture her teeth beyond dental recognition. That would have sent the young detective over the edge. The family would have to see that mess to identify her. It wasn't going to work anyway. The killer couldn't keep her identity a secret that way.

Reconstruction was an art in homicide investigation. However, top labs require money. This was Palm Beach. They had plenty of money. Palm Beach Police Department and Palm Beach County Sheriff's Office Crime Scene Divisions would pick up everything nice and neatly and it would be analyzed.

Analyzed, most likely, at the FBI labs. Influence, money, and power had its privileges. The murder had occurred just a stone toss from Donald Trump's place. He would never sit still for that. The department would get a check.

Seeing a CO_2 cartridge on the ground near the off-road scene, Dr. Ma pointed it out to Detective Brenner. It had been overlooked but most likely, it belonged to the murder victim. It wasn't used. It had probably fallen out of a seat pack, when the bike was knocked over. A necessary piece of equipment wasn't willingly thrown away.

Dr. Ma was a cyclist. She had those cartridges to inflate tires quickly on the road.

Dr. Ma went over the memories she had of the first scene. She knew the killer had targeted the young woman. It couldn't have randomly been someone like her he chose. Dr. Ma couldn't remember ever being the victim of a crime of violence by a human being. "Talk about picking the wrong victim. What a surprise they would get. Now THAT would have been justice," she thought.

David had already picked up on that odd scent from last night. It came from the disparate thread of energy. The one intertwined with, but not the killer's. David bent forward and picked up a handful of sand near the crooked length of chain link fence, separating the island from the parking area.

Dr. Ma walk up next to him and plucked a few leaves off the overhanging tree. She surreptitiously placed them in her mouth and started to chew. David was crumbling the sand in his hand. He brought it up to his nose as if to sniff and casually rubbed it on the side of his cheek.

Ugh! Ma spit her leaves out as David walked to the water quickly to wash his hand.

Oni! Nasty demon smegma taste and smell, they both thought at the same time. "You've got to be kidding me," David whispered fiercely to Dr. Ma. She returned his surprised look with one of her own.

An Oni was an invincible demon or yokai from Japan. What on earth was a trace of energy from such a creature doing here at the murder scene?

Just a trace, but it was unmistakable none-theless, to both Dr. Ma and David. A musky odor was what they smelled, like foul or dead things dragged in and left in a corner to decay.

David had a small personal vendetta against them. The spirit demon was known to wear a tiger skin loincloth when manifesting on the earthly plane. Where they got the skin from, was David's issue.

"What on earth is that thing doing here?" David asked, raising his voice. He was forgetting he was speaking out loud, in hearing range of De-tective Brenner.

Brenner had stepped back to give the two room when he saw what they were doing, but now he stepped forward.
"What thing?" he asked eagerly. His pad and pen were in his hand, poised to take notes. Dr.

Ma was suddenly reminded of Winnie's desk pad calendar. "At least her age lets her be out of touch," Ma thought.

"Best not to ask right now Jeremy," Ma replied very quietly. She looked him directly in the eyes. "This is why you have us here. There is a killer that you will be able to track and take into custody soon enough."

Detective Brenner understood the strong undertone warning him away from further inquiry. He waved to the skiff beached on the small patch of sandy shore to the west of them.

"May I offer you a lift to the crime scene, doctors?" Brenner asked professionally. He knew when to back off and wait for answers to come to him. It was one of his better strengths as an investigator.

Dr. Ma and David walked over to the skiff. They stepped aboard and nodded in unison to the small skiff's Captain. Todd Williams had been the Police Department's sole marine unit officer for years. He had a couple of alternates who often partnered with him on holidays or bad weather. They were also capable of piloting the department's patrol boat.

The skiff was borrowed from Fire Rescue, for this particular operation. Officer Williams, pushed the skiff into the Intracoastal waterway and jumped aboard. In minutes, he was nosing the skiff up against the sole tiny patch of sand, free of roots, on the small islet, that was the final murder scene.

Dr. Ma stepped out of the small skiff as it touched the bit of sandy shore. The rich, metallic scent of fresh blood was no longer present. It had only been there during the first Spirit Wind event.

Now the musky, cloying smell of decay came to her in tendrils on the humid soup of air near the water. South Florida was nothing if not hot and humid in summer.

David and Detective Brenner joined her on the shore after they pulled the nose of the skiff up onto the sand to secure it. There was nobody to steal their only form of transportation here. Possibly a family of raccoons working in concert but it was unlikely they were interested in stealing the skiff.

The four of them were the only human visitors at the murder scene now. The crime scene investigators and the wildlife police had finally left

the scene at peace. Except for the busy raccoons.

Living on the small floating clumps of swampy
sand and plant life was a heavenly opportunity
for a few raccoons. Scrambling over the branch
bridges between islands gave plenty of fishing
in the shallows for current family members and
future generations.

Raccoons were not as territorial when they
were extended family members. The scrub
trees offered nightly shelter and escape routes
when bickering over a morsel became poten-
tially dangerous.

Dr. Ma made note of the creatures as possible
crime scene disruptors. They could easily have
made off with a key piece of evidence before
the police locked the area down with their bags,
and boxes, to cart everything away.
Still present, was that odd thread of another
energetic signature woven through and intimately connected to the one the killer left. The
signature of a Japanese demon spirit. But how
and why was it involved?

Dr. Ma became very still, although her mind
was racing away, putting the odd circumstances
together. Somehow the route the killer took

from his first contact with the victim, was still obscured, until her final moments on the island.

It wasn't that the victim was unconscious and Dr. Ma couldn't see through her eyes how she had been transported, she thought excitedly. The immensely powerful demon spirit had facilitated the killer's path along the island. How else had a simple human passed so easily through the tangles of roots and watery byways carrying someone close to his own body weight?

If the demon had actually carried the woman or helped, that may be why the route from beginning to end was obscured. But why was it here? The signature was faint, just a thread. It didn't make sense yet.

Detective Brenner watched Dr. Ma quietly. David had also gone still, when she had, and was staring at her intently. Brenner knew that they would, soon enough, let him in on their discoveries. He long ago stopped thinking that was at all strange.

Detective Brenner had known both of them for some time now and was not uncomfortable when they exhibited their usual unique skills or odd behaviors. It was, however, one of the thousand reasons he had for keeping their assistance in his cases well under wraps.

"I'm sorry, Jeremy," Dr. Ma apologized. "I know you can't hear me thinking. There is a conspirator involved in this murder we haven't identified yet. I have an idea but you will have to be a bit flexible on the methods used."

"Seriously?" Brenner's eyebrows raised, face showing a look of sarcastic incredulity. "Because up to this point, when it comes to you two, I am pretty by the book and unbending."

They all laughed at that, breaking the atmosphere of the crime scene. "It was all over but for the reckoning," Dr. Ma thought. We are going to catch up with the killer or killers very soon now. "Lets leave this place in peace," she said, moving towards the gently bobbing skiff. Time for nature to reclaim the murder scene and balance to be restored.

They all piled into the skiff and headed along the west shoreline of Bingham Island towards Southern Boulevard. A large raccoon was washing something shiny in the water between two large tree roots. "Stop Captain, please," Ma ordered. The skiff suddenly stilled. "David, would you mind?" she said as she indicated the raccoon.

Following her line of sight, David stood up so gracefully the boat barely moved. Then he jumped lightly out and onto one of the large tree roots nearby. The raccoon scampered away at his approach, dropping its prize.

Reaching down gracefully, David picked up the object carefully with a small evidence bag he had snagged from Detective Brenner's gear. After the thorough washing from the raccoon, there may be little of evidentiary value left.

Captain Miller managed to close his now gaping jaw and nose the skiff closer to where David stood for him to get back onboard. The man was trying to cover his surprise. Neither Detective Brenner nor Dr. Ma seemed to think that David's gravity defying departure from the boat was unusual.

Detective Brenner knew that Dr. Ma could have done the same retrieval with as much or more skill than David. She most likely used the lithe and powerful young man to reduce the shock factor for the Captain.

David settled lightly into the skiff and handed Detective Brenner the plastic evidence bag containing a small metal wallet. Brenner could see the victim's drivers license was inside and half chewed, effectively wedging it in the slender opening.

"Well that takes the guess work out of identifying her," Brenner said. "Even with the facial damage, that is going to be her, I'll bet. Susan Miller. We have you now, dear."

Brenner had a habit of talking to murder victims as if they could hear him. It gave him a measure of comfort to think they knew he was going to solve their case. He felt they all deserved a measure of justice for what they had suffered.

"Thanks docs," Brenner said as they all stepped out of the skiff, now back on the causeway beach area. "As usual, I couldn't do it all without you."

"I will be in touch, Jeremy," Ma replied, acknowledging his thanks with a nod of her head.

Dr. Ma and David walked back to their car as Detective Brenner placed his new evidence in the lock box of his unmarked police car.

"David?" Brenner called. David turned and looked back at him.

"Yes?" David replied.

"The ladies group from the Four Arts that hosted the Defense Strategies for Women class last year, has specifically requested you take over again." Brenner said this with a barely suppressed smile.

David had assisted, or actually taken over last year from one of their officers. The officer who taught the class every year was retiring, and nobody else had the time and expertise to teach.

Fees from the class went to the Annual Awards Dinner and Dance for the Palm Beach Police Department. David had volunteered his time and drawn rave reviews.

The ladies had circumvented any change back to a police department instructor this year, with a letter to the Chief, requesting David come back for a reprisal.

"The class has pre-registration at fifty right now, you will have to split it into two sessions," Brenner teased.

Smiling, David shook his head and turned back to Ma's car. She had it running, waiting for him. She couldn't listen to the exchange without laughing. "Anything for charity," David called over his shoulder.

"Check!" Brenner thought. "I can tell the Chief today." One thing more off the list, and brownie points banked at the same time.

Since it was Detective Brenner, who had arranged for the very successful free instructor, last year, the Chief of Police had credited him when the ladies group gave their glowing reviews.

Chapter Eight - Just Another Day

The next day brought more patients, and an intense discussion, about the crime when they had breaks. Detective Brenner had called earlier and said he was making notification to Susan's husband today. Allen Miller had reported his wife missing when she didn't come home from her bike ride the night of the murder.

This time, Winnie sat in to give her perspective. "Who kills to steal a bicycle and a backpack with a few bucks and some bike gear?" Winnie asked Dr. Ma and David.

"Someone perhaps desperate and depraved," Dr. Ma answered.

"But what is with the major effort to hide the body and her identity?" Winnie countered. "That seems planned out."

Dr. Ma smiled. She enjoyed baiting Winnie and getting her bare bones perspective. "As a rule, depravity doesn't exclude pre-planning, but desperation does."

Dr. Ma had a pervasive feeling that the homeless man was a puppet on some complex and hidden strings. "One thing at a time," she thought. "Find the killer first. That was a major puzzle piece. Fit it into the big picture, and other smaller pieces would fit as well."

David was thinking along the same lines. "So, who or what, lures off the street, beats and kills a young woman he has never met? An Ma, Do you have a solid read on this one?" He used a old name for her. Never having heard it before, Winnie looked at him for an explanation. Not wanting to get off track, David ignored her unspoken question.

An Ma, a private name for Dr. Ma he used at times through the years. *An*, meant peace. Not exactly the peace you think of as in, no conflict peace. The name meant, bringer of peace. No judgement on the method of bringing said peace.

Skipping lunch today, Dr. Ma and David had met briefly with Detective Brenner in Palm Beach to look over the forensic evidence that the Town of Palm Beach, and the Palm Beach County Sheriff's Office had collected.

Evidence that led nowhere at this moment.They had agreed to use their time off to gather evidence from their personal sources. Hopefully the vagrant had tried to sell the murder victim's bike.

A vagrant, shouldn't have that bike. That was a precious possession to a serious cyclist. Like a finger print, bikes like that bore identifiers to local mechanics and other riders.

"Her murder had been made public, so you can't own her bike." Ma was talking to the unidentified killer as she mused out loud "You can't get rid of the evidence and profit from it. You thought she may never be found. You were almost right."

Winnie cleared her throat. She hated long silences while everyone thought deep thoughts but her. She wanted to see action on this case. "What is the plan now?" she asked.

"Dr. Ma and I need to identify him. Rather, Dr. Ma does," David said quickly, correcting his error.

"I could identify him clearly on sight at this point," Ma replied. "I don't know exactly where to find him. Can you go back to the scene, David, and try to pick up a trail for us to track him directly?"

Winnie silently raised her eyebrows, but didn't say anything when Dr. Ma said she could identify the killer by site. Years of working with Dr. Ma and David gave her everything but proof that the two were not normal folks ,in so many ways. "How would she know what he looked like?" Winnie thought. "One day you will find out, don't ask now."

Winnie looked at David, as he stood a little straighter, squared his broad shoulders, and answered Dr. Ma.

"Of course I can," David replied confidently. "Maybe we will get lucky and Brenner will get some technical forensic break, and it's done before we have to get more involved,".

Dr. Ma smiled back grimly. "I don't see that as the path ahead. I could be wrong, things can always change. It's just that there is a glitch in why the murder was actually committed by our bad guy that I can't see beyond."

David regarded her seriously a moment, before replying. Ma was never wrong even if she wasn't exactly right at this moment. "I'll go back after class tonight and let you know what I find."

"I am going to follow the trail of the bike, so to say," Ma replied. "I will take the afternoon off and do some checking."

"Is there a possibility our killer will leave the area?" David asked.

"No," Dr. Ma replied. "He is somehow imbedded in this time and place. I didn't feel fear, regret, anxiety or anything I would have expected it in the aura impression left behind. It's as if he didn't completely register what he did during, or after, the act."

Winnie tried, but failed, to follow the entire line of Dr. Ma's thinking. It was never easy.

"Complications" David grinned. "Brenner is going to cross you off his Christmas list for sure this year."

Dr. Ma gave him a broad smile, enjoying the reference to Detective Brenner's consternation at her valuable input in his cases.

"What, no vegan fruitcake for us?" she laughed.

"Wait! Please, no vegan fruitcake again this year. What was that mess he found for us last year?" David said.

"Are you kidding? You ate the whole thing," Ma replied. "I didn't think it was even digestible yet I saw no negative effect on you."

At this point Winnie let out a loud guffaw. That was her version of hysterical laughter. David frowned in her direction.

"You know I can digest about anything," David said seriously. "I also can't stand to see food go to waste. Even poorly prepared, or in this case, ill-conceived attempts at fruitcake."

"Yes, of course, no food goes to waste in your world," Dr. Ma commented.

David took over the remainder of the afternoon patients while Dr. Ma went off to investigate.

Two healing foot fractures, sciatica, and a chronic migraine sufferer were among a few simple walk-ins. David could have summed it up by saying "Use proper shoes" (foot fracture), "what I just said" (foot fracture), "lose weight and stretch" (sciatica) and "stop eating coffee and chocolate" (migraine) "when you know it triggers headaches." All said in that order.

Instead, he would give each patient time to express their concerns, listening to every detail. Then the patient would participate in crafting a plan for care today, and in the future. After that, a meticulous physical exam would be followed by a caring and compassionate treatment.

David and Dr. Ma worked on the same patient-centered principles, but were vastly different in methodology. David handled one patient for every two to three patients Dr. Ma treated. It was a perfect blend.

David usually handled the non-athlete referrals and difficult cases. Dr. Ma breezed through the athletes and routine followups in record time. They both collaborated on diagnoses, as needed.

After leaving Winnie and David to handle the afternoon workload, Dr. Ma drove north on I95 to Okeechobee Boulevard. She continued west to the bike shop that she had patronized for years. Tam, the owner, was a friend. He was also a halfbreed.

Halfbreed's were a mix of otherworldly beings and humans. They were not common. For the most part, conception didn't occur no matter what happened. Even the relationship between the otherworldly and the human didn't last long. Too many intrinsic differences made this a difficult situation, at best.

Dr. Ma had always wondered how Tam, re-mained relatively unknown, to the human world around him. He was a bit aloof, but kind and compassionate. His presence in the local bike community was wide-spread. He involved him-self in everything from races to education, and recently, public thoroughfare legislation for bike travel lanes and rider safety.

Tam also drank a bit. Dr. Ma knew it was a form of self medication. There was some emo-tional and physical discomfort involved in choosing one or the other worlds, when you kind of belonged to both. In fact, pretty much all the halfbreed's she knew, somewhat heavily self medicated.

Tam's shop was in western West Palm Beach off the busy main highway, and tucked back into an obscure area behind a military supply store. He said he couldn't afford more rent than he paid to remain in the shabby area he had been at for decades. "Probably right," she thought. Bike sales and repairs weren't a high money maker. Tam's prices were always fair, too, and he did much for the community at no cost to promote cycling.

"Hey, Dr. Ma!" Tam greeted her as she entered the tidy but overflowing shop. "You planning on riding the Loop around the Lake this year?"

"With my schedule? You never know," Ma replied smiling. Two local cyclists were just leaving as she walked up to the counter. Tam was behind the counter in the repair area, and for the moment they were alone.

"I am looking for someone," Dr. Ma said.

Tam kept working on the bike he had up on the stand. "I heard," he replied.

Ma knew he got information like she did. Birds, trees, odd otherworldly creatures, and more were his sources. Tam was a veteran mountain biker. He easily kept in touch with his other-worldly contacts, while riding off road.

"Do you know where he is now?" she asked. "I know he manipulated the killer, the police are going to arrest. I need to trap the shadow that was actually pulling the strings."

Tam looked at her, his normally hazel eyes, changing briefly to the deep blue of all other-worldly beings. Tam was half human half wind spirit so he and Dr. Ma shared a deep affinity. All dragons were wind creatures.

"They have been following him all day," Tam replied. "You will find him tonight in Lake Worth, by Brian Park.

Dr. Ma regarded him quietly for a moment. "Thank you, wind child," she said. Tam's eyes flashed blue again briefly. "We cannot let these evil ones do as they please. It appears to be Oni."

Tam curled his lip and flared his nostrils as if he was smelling something bad. Wind spirits didn't like the nasty smelling demons either. The creatures could leave their stink in a location for days after passing by. Wind spirits were particularly sensitive to bad smells.

"No, we can't," Tam replied quietly and turned back to the bicycle he was repairing. He looked up again and curled his upper lip. "I thought I could smell that on the messenger when he told me he found him."

Dr. Ma nodded her thanks again and walked to the front door. Tam's partner was coming in with a box of donuts. "Donut?" he offered Dr. Ma. She laughed, "You guys are like giant trash cans when it comes to food."

"True!" he said. "I have fresh ground coffee." He waved a bag of coffee beans temptingly.

"Another time, but thank you." Dr. Ma replied.

"Make you faster on the road," he said. Ma just smiled and shook her head as she left.

When Dr. Ma returned to the clinic, she shared her findings with David. "I think we need to get our information from the killer tonight if the Air Spirits have his location locked down. Usual time?" Ma asked David.
"I'll meet you in the median on the west side of the bridge," David replied. Usual time." he confirmed.

"Sounds like a plan," Ma smiled.

David had yet another charity event on Palm Beach island again tonight, so Dr. Ma took over the dojo's class schedule that evening.

"Be good," Ma called after David as he opened the back door to leave. He still had to get home and dress for the event. Black tie was easy for him. Certain pieces were required, not much thinking went into it. All in all, not much different than his martial arts attire.

"Will do," he replied. Dr. Ma kept David's gaze a moment, neither of them speaking out loud. "Be safe my friend," she thought. "I sense someone's attention on you this evening." David nodded to her half in acknowledgment and half in appreciation. She was never wrong. "Who knows what the night will bring with it?" he thought.

Dr. Ma taught the classes and went home for a quick bite to eat before laying down for one of her sleepless rest periods. She would be the one to encounter the Oni tonight if it was attached to the killer. David would hold everything in stasis if she needed to fight or destroy the demon.

That kind of work required a large energy expenditure from her human form. One of the reasons to keep it so fit and healthy! She only hoped David would get some quality rest.

The installation dinner David attended that night, at the Colony Hotel, went well. As a large donor, David had been invited to the Board of Directors' Black Tie Dinner. *Save the Tigers,* Allistair had teased him when he saw the check David had written at the benefit. "Did that come with a mate? That was how David could save the tigers," Allistair joked.

David spent several hours talking to a young woman at the benefit. She was also a new board member. He found himself oddly attracted to her. "She *smelled* intriguing," he thought. She quickly attached herself to him when he had arrived tonight. Quite a few jealous looks came from the various women in the room. David ignored anything but her. Karen was her name.

After the dinner, she asked if she could drive him home. She noticed he had arrived with two other guests who were still talking. Karen hoped David would be ready to leave early. He accepted her ride and didn't seem surprised when she pulled up, instead, in front of what he assumed was her own house.

Saying nothing, Karen walked David through the vast marble entry of her parents' Palm Beach home and upstairs to the suite that had been hers since they moved to the island 10 years ago.

He seemed rather gentle and a bit shy despite his incredible good looks. She had been sure he would be a player. She closed the door behind them and started to undress him, eager to see more.

She was not disappointed as she revealed his muscular torso. There were beautiful tattoos surrounding his waist and pelvis and diving down his tight lean flanks. She noticed he blushed slightly as she partly tugged his pants off his hips.

Stepping back quickly, she slipped off the elegant cocktail dress she wore, dropping it carelessly to the floor. Karen wore a silk and lace slip with nothing underneath. She noticed his desire in the look he gave her, but with another hint of shyness, he looked away briefly.

Karen was intrigued even more than before. As David gently embraced her she felt an overwhelming sense of sheer physical power coming from him.

She also felt a strange fear rising in her as they kissed. The fear reminded her of what she felt when she had been very close to wild animals in Africa. It was exhilaration from the sheer proximity of a dangerous animal. An animal that could kill you easily. She was looking at him directly when he raised his eyes to hers.

"He senses my fear," she thought. "No, that's irrational, only animals sense fear like that."

David did sense her fear. He was still holding her. He was trying hard to rein in his response to her. Everything had to be very controlled. To keep her safe from him. There was no other way to be with a human. Control.

It was then that he felt it. Her recoiling from him. There was that innate ability of a human to sense a predator. "She wouldn't understand why," he thought. "They never do. They just go from desire to panic."

Karen watched David's expression change slightly. He released his embrace of her and she saw a glimpse, yes just a fleeting moment of sadness as he stepped back from her. Unable to move or say anything to him at that moment, she felt frozen like a rabbit caught in headlights. It was fear.

David nodded to her as if to some unanswered question from her unmoving lips. He turned and picked up his scattered clothing, dressing quickly. She wanted to speak or move but her mouth and limbs were not responding. The fear had frozen her. "It was so confusing, he doesn't look frightening," she thought. "What was going on?"

David slipped out the door of her suite, and moments later she heard the big front door close softly. She still hadn't moved.

Walking quickly, he headed towards the Intracoastal to clear his head. The soft breezes and sounds of the waterway at night were soothing. He sat on the concrete abutment near the line of moored luxury yachts. The Palm Beach docks were quiet this time of evening.

He thought of their murder victim, Susan. "We will get him tonight." He wouldn't have had much time tonight with Karen, even if things had worked out. They had a killer to put away.

A soft splash beside him revealed one of the water Sprites that lived in the Intracoastal Waterway. Then another, and another, popped up to stare at him. David stared back silently.

The full moon was bright tonight in a cloudless sky. The first Sprite regarded his attire and pointed, chuckling in its metallic little voice. "Whoever said they laughed like bells ringing was crazy," David thought, "more like out-of-tune tin cans, really."

"Trying to mate out of your *species* again, tiger?" the Sprite taunted him. "Too bad humans can smell the predator on you even in those fancy clothes." The other sprites laughed with the first one.

"Not tonight, creature," David growled softly in warning. He was in no mood to be teased. "But wait," David thought. "How would you know?" The memory of her open terrace windows, facing the Intracoastal Waterway where the creatures lived, came back to him in vivid detail. The whole scenario between him and Karen would have easily been witnessed by the Sprites. He felt anger rising.

"Foolish cat, playing with your food," the Sprite taunted. These were a group of young Sprites, and not very smart to tease him in the first place. Quick as any cat and more powerful, David hooked the offending Sprite by its scruff, dangling it in the air. There wasn't even a drop of water on his tuxedo, he moved so fast.

The Sprites' screams of terror drew an adult Sprite near to the abutment. "Put him down, Great Cat," the older Sprite said softly, but with authority. "He is just a child and doesn't know better."

David growled softly, shaking the young Sprite before setting him back into the water. The terrified creature disappeared into the depths of the Intracoastal waterway.

"I am sorry to frighten him, Elder," David said apologetically.

"No, we must apologize to you," the older Sprite said bowing to him. "I know your pain, Great Cat. To live alone among humans who desire and fear you at the same time must be very sad," the Sprite said.

David didn't comment but nodded to acknowledge the Sprite's attempt at comfort. Tonight was just a long line of failures interacting with humans. Sure, sometimes he even managed at least one evening, but it never lasted long. Sexual intimacy with him and a human being was overwhelming for them, and less than adequate for him anyway.

"Great Cat," the Sprite began, not wanting to interrupt his train of thought.

"Yes, Elder?"

"We have news of the dark shadow that killed the female," the Sprite said proudly.

David started "What? We are about to have the killer in jail."

The Sprite Elder looked around nervously. "You have the vehicle of death, not the driver."

David stepped forward eagerly, sending the nervous Sprite fleeing into the water. "No! Please! I'm sorry to frighten you. Come back!" David quickly sat back on the abutment to show the Sprite he meant it no harm.

The Elder Sprite swam back slowly, eyeing David carefully. "It was a mere shadow, the human form that held it was not here. We saw it follow the vagrant you sought and it carried him over the island to where he left the woman's body."

"Thank you, Elder, I will share this with Ma-sama tonight. This is very important," David said. He kept his excitement down, staying still so as not to startle the little creature again.

The Sprite nodded and slipped away into the moonlit waterway. David rose slowly. His powerful cat eyes noted that the dock master was sound asleep at her post. "Good thing," he thought. She couldn't see the Sprites but she could see him acting like an idiot in evening clothes.

David made it home in record time and quickly changed out of his tuxedo. Typical dojo training gear would be proper attire for the rest of the night. He would be expected to provide Dr. Ma a safe space to deal with the Oni if it showed up.

Chapter Nine - To Catch A Killer

That night, Dr. Ma and David found the vagrant who killed Susan Miller easily enough. He still had the stench of Oni demon gently woven in the fabric of his outer clothing. He also hadn't strayed far from the crime scene. Yet.

Jack was his name. They had heard several other homeless men call to him as he walked by them. They wouldn't have heard them, if both hadn't possessed the hearing of high level predators. Even in their human guise.

The two Elementals were at the east end of the Lake Worth Bridge. A small heavily planted median split the traffic going east and west on the bridge, and provided a splash of greenery and vibrant color from tropical flowers.

Watching him, as Jack moved in and around the homeless camp in Brian Park, neither Dr. Ma nor David saw any sign of the Oni demon. The one that had such an awful smell. "I can't believe humans can't pick up on that stench," Ma said.

David wrinkled his nose in disgust. "Neither can I, really," He moved slowly away from their position behind the median foliage. "I guess we can let Jeremy pick this guy up now."

Dr. Ma followed David towards the golf course fencing on the north side of the bridge, "I have a plan," she said. "Let's help Detective Brenner pick up Jack and then invite the demon and his human transportation to come here to the homeless camp."

David regarded her silently. His eyes glowed softly from the yellow ring around the lapis blue iris. Dr. Ma's eyes were a copy of his. They only glowed in the dark when the two Elementals needed the ability to see like nocturnal predators.

"Were you planning on a formal invitation or an email one?" he asked deadpan. "I will have to extract his address from Jack once he is arrested."

Dr. Ma slipped her inside leg in front of his as they walked, suddenly stopping and leaning into his mid body. David went down fast as Ma planned, but agile cat that he was, he twisted in mid air and rolled, landing again on his feet. "Annoying creature!" Ma said.

They both laughed and silently hopped over the chainlink fence of the golf course. More like moving smoke than walking humans, they headed towards the Intracoastal and the Snook Islands. The Snook Islands were small circular fisheries dotting the East side of the golf course. Man made, they were an attempt to restore the Eco system of the Lake Worth Lagoon.

A water Sprite popped up as they neared the East bank. "Ma-sama!" the older Sprite greeted Dr. Ma. "Great tiger!" the creature added. "Have a nice talk with the Brian Park alternative housing residents?"

Dr. Ma grinned. "Everyone is a comedian tonight." She enjoyed the humor, it kept things from getting overly tense in these situations. "I need to know something, Elder," she addressed the Sprite respectfully.

"Not a problem," the little creature replied. He stepped up on the bank, eyeing David carefully. Sprites seemed to fear the tiger, even in his human manifestation.
"David will not harm you in any way," Dr. Ma reassured the Sprite. "Be still please," she admonished her companion. David was pacing a

bit restlessly behind her. He, begrudgingly, sat on the bank next to her with a slight frown.

"Take this to Jack for me," Dr. Ma asked the Sprite. The little creature nodded in agreement and slipped back into the waterway.

Dr. Ma knelt by the water and slipped her right hand below the surface. Closing her eyes, she spun a delicate silvery thread of consciousness into the waterway from her fingertips. The Sprite grasped the end of the delicate thread and swam rapidly south along the Intracoastal bank and under the bridge.

"I'll give a tug when he bites," the Sprite called over its shoulder, as it disappeared from sight.

"No need, really," David growled softly, watching the creature move south. "We can both see you as if it was daylight."

"Shhh," Dr. Ma reminded him and settled in to wait, eyes closed and breathing slowing as she concentrated.
The Sprite swam up to the concrete wall separating Brian Park from the Intracoastal. Like he was using a fishing lure, he tossed the thread of Dr. Ma's consciousness up and over the concrete and dangled it there temptingly.

The Sprite began to sing a tinny sounding tune. Tinny to the ears of otherworldly beings, but quite lovely to human ears. This time he was only singing to one human. Jack, the killer.

Jack was shuffling along the shell rock pathway that skirted the barrier wall. He had been doing this for several hours while Dr. Ma and David watched him. The dangling thread of consciousness would have appeared like something he wanted, something he would surreptitiously go over to investigate.

Jack walked up and reached out for the dangling silvery thread, or whatever he saw it to be in his head. As he touched the delicate filament, he bridged the connection between himself, the Sprite, and Dr. Ma. The water simply served as a rapid conduit of energy.

"There you go, dragon," the Sprite said tugging slightly on the thread. It fixed its gaze on Jack, with its hypnotic eyes and said, "There you go Jackie, it's pretty isn't it?"

Jack nodded and agreed "Yes, pretty!"

"You want to stay here with me and watch it don't you Jackie," the Sprite said.

"Watch it," Jack agreed.

Dr. Ma was pulling thoughts and memories from Jack, like sipping from a straw. She was sorting rapidly, looking for the information she wanted before something could interrupt her process. "Ah! Got it," she said.

David turned to her. "All done?" he inquired. She nodded, pushing all the thoughts and memories back down the silvery line to their owner. David reached out and snapped the thread between two of his fingers. The connection was gone.

"Argh!" the two of them heard the Sprite scream as he tumbled off the concrete barrier. The little creature had been holding the tension on the line connecting to Jack. David suddenly cutting it, caused him to tumble into the water unceremoniously. "I. Really. Hate. Cats," came bubbling up from below the surface.

David looked chagrined. "Sorry?" he offered. There was no response from the Sprite.

Dr. Ma got up from the ground, and headed north again along the embankment. "He will forgive you, David," she said. "Come on, I know what we have to do now to catch the creature who orchestrated this murder."

David followed her reluctantly, looking back over his shoulder periodically. He really wanted to apologize to the Sprite. He seemed to always be at odds with the little creatures.

Dr. Ma and David made it to her home that evening, in record time. "Stay here tonight, David," she said to him. "I am sure the Oni saw me looking at it through Jack's eyes. I don't know whether it will seek Jack out tonight or tomorrow, but one of us should rest while the other watches.

David nodded his agreement and took the first watch.

The next morning, while it was still dark, they ran Dr. Ma's usual route together. Then, they showered and changed for work. There was always several changes of clothing at either of their residences for the other to spend the night. The only thing Dr. Ma had to worry about when David stayed over was the loss of every-thing edible in the house. The tiger had a vora-cious appetite.

Her expression grim, Ma got into her car with David and called Detective Brenner. It had been too late the night before to disturb him, and no need.

"Meet me in Lake Worth for breakfast at Blue-Jays Restaurant," she said. "I have another killer for you to catch."

Brenner muffled his surprise at her statement and grunted an agreement. "It'll take me about 20," he said.

"I'm coming from home, with David," she said, giving him her general location. "That should work out fine. Jeremy?"

"Yes Dr. Ma?"

"Clear your evening please. This is going to be a long day."

Dr. Ma heard Detective Brenner sigh as he hung up. She drove south towards downtown Lake Worth. They arrived at the same time as Brenner.

David stayed outside to call Winnie, and make sure his morning class had gone smoothly. He had texted Jet last night and she agreed to handle it.

Dr. Ma and Detective Brenner had just settled in to the furthest back booth along the window,when David walked up. He settled in next to Jeremy facing Dr. Ma.

Jeremy Brenner was a man's man, an old-fashioned Irish kid, with a drop of German that gave him his surname. He had never understood homosexuality on a personal level. He accepted, without judgement, the ever increasing population of gay men and women in Palm Beach. It didn't effect him in the least as far as he was concerned. Everyone deserved the best job he could do. Everyone deserved compassion and consideration whether you understood their choices or not.

Despite all this, he moved away from David as the stunning young man slipped into the booth next to him. Jeremy was aware of the jealous looks from the gay male waiters and patrons. He had looked up when David came in. Brenner sat facing west. Facing the door of the restaurant as any good cop should. He had tracked David's rapid pace through the maze of waiters and patrons in the small spaces between the tables and booths.

Women looked at David as he passed, men looked at David as he passed. Brenner, uncomfortably understood their interest. He always felt an odd, almost sexual response when David was very close or touching him. Dr. Ma also created a response when she was close or touched him during training at the dojo. This seemed more normal to him.

Dr. Ma was a beautiful woman. Jeremy was taught that being interested in beautiful women was normal. He didn't know what to make of the feelings David engendered in him, and didn't want to know. Based on the looks Jeremy just witnessed, plenty of others knew what to make of David.

Jeremy noticed covert looks of admiration when he passed with Dr. Ma, but somehow those were different. The men and women quickly looked away again. Most still had their tongues hanging out of their mouths in David's direction. Thank goodness David and Ma were oblivious and focused on their conversation.

Detective Brenner brought himself back to what Dr. Ma was saying.

"We can pick him up tonight, Jeremy," Ma said. She nodded out of the window to her left. Dr. Ma sat with her back to the door facing east.

Detective Brenner knew that the time span in her reaction if something or someone came through that door and presented a danger, was infinitely faster than he could ever hope to respond. He had trained with her for years. He felt they had the safety of the restaurant pretty well covered at this point.

Add David and it was a slam dunk in their favor.

The Lake Worth Town Square was to Dr. Ma's left across the street from the restaurant. This was the local gathering place for homeless people and what Brenner referred to as vagrants. "Not the same thing," Brenner thought. "Homeless was a blanket term for everyone these days."

Some homeless were vagrants, preferring the life out of doors, no ties, no bills, panhandling, and petty crime. Some were just regular folk down on their luck and temporarily living in the open. Then there was the population of addicts that clustered around the homeless groups and camps for support and sometimes protection from local criminals who liked to prey on them.

"He hasn't left the area, Jeremy," Ma said, still looking out the window, at the small concrete square. A large and beautiful tree once stood on the south side of the plaza. It shaded a large area of the square for years providing a small ecosystem for birds, tiny reptiles and insects.

It had been cut down several years ago in a misunderstood and perhaps misguided attempt to protect the public from falling limbs. The tree, you see, had been aging less than gracefully. The email had requested the tree be trimmed. The interpretation was 'cut it down if you think trimming won't do the trick.'

Ma had known that tree. Not a Sentinel like Jamil, just a tree spirit. Tam had told her about the tree's death. He had been with the Tuesday bike night ride at the base of the Lake Worth Bridge, when the displaced air spirits had gathered around him, distraught and homeless themselves. Air spirits often use large trees to anchor themselves to the Earth. It is them who make the soft music in the tree limbs everyone seems to attribute to winds.

"Too bad," Ma thought. That tree would have helped us tonight. She would just have to introduce herself to the tree on the opposite side of the square. He wasn't as friendly in appearance. He sheltered the collection of homeless, vagrants, and addicts, under his deep canopy during the day and obscured the actions of local drug dealers that used his dark shadows at night.

"Regardless," Ma thought, "that is where the vagrant killer would be in a few hours as the sunset faded on the east side of the bridge by the ocean."
Ma continued giving information to Detective Brenner.

"One of the local cyclists, who saw your killer with the dead woman's bike, told us he makes his home here, Jeremy." Ma looked back at Detective Brenner now, reluctantly it seemed, taking her gaze away from the square. She used the cyclist witness, to avoid explaining more of her and David's investigation. She also couldn't explain Tam's involvement to Detective Brenner.

"The local cyclist asked around and said the man's name is Jack Daniels Kelly," she added. "Do you have enough forensic evidence to connect him to the victim's death?" Dr. Ma didn't like to say Susan's or any victim's name. "It almost seemed to tug the spirit back to the Earthly plane when you invoked their name over and over. Hence the significant amount of haunting in theaters, courtrooms and libraries," she thought.

"The spirit could of course ignore you if they wished," Ma reflected. "It's just that some of them leave reluctantly and don't find their path to the next manifestation easily. They remain within earshot and drift back towards the sound of their names from habit."

"I will have the Palm Beach County Sheriff's office deputies with me," Detective Brenner said. "They know all the locals. I'll ask about a guy named Kelly first thing."

"What does he look like now?" David asked Ma.

Brenner looked up. "Did you see the sketch?" he asked.

"No," David replied still looking at Dr. Ma. "I was interested to know if he changed his appearance." This was an important point.

"No changes," Ma answered. "It is as if he has no idea he did anything wrong. He isn't hiding at all."

Detective Brenner paid the check for their coffee and the three parted until later. They would meet at dusk, with the rest of the operational personnel, several blocks north of downtown to avoid suspicion.

Dr. Ma dropped David off at the clinic to treat today's patients and keep Winnie in the loop. "I will pick you up later," she said.

Sometimes before an encounter with a demon they didn't know well, Ma would consult resources in the library she and Allistair kept for that reason. It was not a place on this plane of existence. You could only get to it as an Elemental who could travel in spirit form away from their physical body. David knew that was where she was headed now.

David grinned at her. "See you soon, have a safe trip." Ma smiled and drove away.

Breezing in the back door and startling Winnie who was just coming out of an exam room, he gave her a quick peck on the cheek. "Morning," he said as he ducked her swat towards him.

"I have cleared almost everything you two had on the schedule today," Winnie said. She tried to glare at him. "Are the police going to catch the killer today?"

"I believe so Winnie," he said. "Did you do anything about class tonight?"
"Not yet," she said. "I'm glad you two are almost finished with the case. The clinic is going to hell in a hand basket with all the time you two take off." He grinned at her and walked into his office to make some calls.

David quickly arranged for their most senior student to take the evening class from him. Winnie was all abustle around the office. Her barely contained excitement at the new developments in the case, were amusing. "The woman just loved a mystery," David thought.

"Winnie?" David called her as the day of patients quickly ended. Dr. Ma would be picking him up soon. The day was fading to dusk. He walked into her domain, the front office and pharmacy She looked up at him, eyebrows raised in a silent question.

"Yes, Dr. Anderson," she replied formally. David noticed that a woman was sitting with her back to him in the waiting area. He thought everyone had gone for the day. He looked back at Winnie and raised his eyebrows in the same type of silent question.

Winnie simply nodded at him, and then at the woman sitting with her back to him. David frowned and walked into the reception area. Apparently the visitor was for him. As he walked around to see the visitor from the front, he stopped suddenly as if running, into a glass wall.

Winnie watched the whole situation unfold carefully. She was the ever protective mother figure, and would gladly throw the pretty young woman out on her backside if she was here to cause trouble for David.

Karen looked up at David hesitantly and smiled. David, so far, hadn't said anything. He looked somewhat shocked to see her. "I found out where your clinic was, so I could come by and tell you how very sorry I am, about last night" she said. Karen carefully eyed Winnie as she spoke to him.

"Is there somewhere we could speak privately?" Karen asked him.

"Not really," David answered. Their computer tech was in his office updating the equipment so he was being very truthful.

David stretched a hand out towards the reception couch. "Please sit here. May I get you some tea?" The clinic had a nice tea bar on a table next to the sitting area. "I am going to have a cup myself." David tried to cover his surprise at seeing her, by busying himself making a cup of macha tea.

"No, thank you," Karen replied. "I enjoyed meeting you and spending time together the other night, would you consider coming over for dinner tonight?"

David splashed a few fat drops of hot water on his hand holding the cup, as this surprising invitation settled in. He made no show of the pain in his hand as he finished preparing his tea. "I'm afraid tonight is not good" he said.

Karen's face fell as if she expected his refusal. "Tomorrow night then?" she asked hopefully.

David got the impression she was not going to let him off the hook until he agreed. "Sounds possible. Or perhaps the next night, if that works for you. Would you leave you number, so

I can get in touch with you if I have any patient emergencies?"

"Certainly," Karen replied, handing him her personal card. "Again, my apologies, I hope we can end a different night, on a better note." She smiled and brushed past him to leave without looking back.

David looked up to see Winnie giving him the 'look'. "Stop that," David rebuked her.

"She is hot stuff," Winnie replied. "Where did that one come from, and is she trying to apologize for something I may want to speak with her about privately?"

David smiled to himself. Winnie gave him such a hard time and yet was incredibly protective of him. Her children didn't live locally, and he always assumed, he was her surrogate child.

A memory of the woman who had raised him in this lifetime teased the edge of his consciousness. She had been kind, but she hadn't protected him. She let things run their course when her husband had been in the mood to take his anger out on David.

The sound of Dr. Ma's Mercedes horn outside, pulled him back to the present.

"Coming," David responded, to nobody. He shook his head, clearing the memories he wished he could forget. "Ok Winnie," he called to their clinic manager. "I have to go with Dr. Ma and meet Detective Brenner. Can you take over from here?"

"Please," Winnie replied sarcastically. "As if your presence here made things run smoothly."

David smiled at her, and tossed his white lab coat into his office, before hurrying out the back door.

Winnie, following behind him, bent and picked the coat up before hanging it on the back of the door. She had installed big hooks on each of the doctors doors some time ago, but still found David's lab coats anywhere he tossed them. The computer tech smiled and shook his head.

A couple of hours later, Dr. Ma and David were casually strolling down the sidewalk bordering the square in Lake Worth. Detective Brenner was positioned at a bench outside of BlueJays in his workout gear to blend in.

"He still looks like a cop," Ma observed to David.

"Yep," David replied grinning. "How do these guys catch anyone? I can smell his soap and aftershave from here." They were about 100 feet away from Detective Brenner at this point.

"Good question," Ma answered. "Thank goodness the bad guys don't all have your sense of smell."

David, admonished, didn't reply. Ma suddenly squeezed David's arm. "He is at the base of the bridge, coming this way."

Dr. Ma and David moved quickly to a position next to the large tree on the north side of the square. They were going to prevent the big tree from obscuring any of the officer's vision, as they arrested their suspect.

Trees didn't have powerful magic but they could stir their tree spirits and cause some strange visual effects. When Dr. Ma had introduced herself to the tree earlier and asked for its co-operation, she had been refused. None too politely. Too bad. Now she would use her and David's much more powerful abilities to keep the tree from interfering.

Jack Daniels Kelly walked slowly towards the Lake Worth Town Square. He had spent the day in Brian Park talking to his buddies who were also homeless.

Brian Park and the Square were conveniently located near BlueJays Deli,as well as the parking area, where the St. Andrews Church volunteers, brought them dinner every night. You could get free soda and coffee from BlueJays twice a day if you were polite and didn't smell too bad.

Dinner was a good gig right now, but Jack always picked up his, and anyone else's styrofoam containers, if they dropped them instead of putting them in the big trash bin.

Jack had lived other places where handouts had been banned due to the crazy's that seemed to migrate towards the homeless camps. Addicts, alcoholics and crazies, he thought. They were who ruined it for the rest of us.

Jack hadn't always lived on the street. He grew up in a trailer park west of Town. His mother, an alcoholic, had never married his father, another drinker and rage-a-holic. Jack had lived with them long enough to know he never wanted a family. He never wanted to be in the same place more than a month or so at a time, really. Jack wandered from camp to camp. He had been in Brian Park a few months now. Almost time to go.

Something had happened about a week ago that left Jack wondering if he had already over-stayed this place. He remembered talking to a man near the base of the bridge. The man had offered him a ride somewhere. Jack just couldn't remember where. The last thing he clearly remembered was getting into the man's car.

Jack liked cars and this was a nice one. Mercedes sedan, newer model and black, real shiny. Then he remembered waking up in his tent the next day in Brian Park. His buddy Jimmy said he was gone until early in the morning and the same car as took him and his cart away, brought him back.
Jimmy didn't sleep so good on account of his arthritis so he heard and saw a lot. He was the first to alert anyone in the camp to kids poking around for trouble. Or worse.

Jack saw the big tree coming that draped over the sidewalk. His buddies were all converging there for a good chat, and to share some weed and beer before they wandered off for the night. Dinner had been fried chicken and mashed potatoes from the church. Everyone had cleaned their plates. Now for social time.

Jack walked up, shouldering his ratty backpack. He had found $50 in it the morning after the stranger had picked him up. He figured it was for whatever he did for the man. "God, he hoped he hadn't done nothin' freaky," he thought. He couldn't remember, like back when he was drinking so bad. This time he couldn't tell you why he didn't remember, but he hoped the $50 was for something legit.

Jack saw Deputy Sheriff Bonnie Thomas coming across the square in his direction. She smiled like she always did. Jack liked her, she was nice to him. Still, his instincts told him to turn around. Or was it the tree? Jack often thought the tree talked to him. Of course he was crazy, wasn't he? Too much alcohol in his life, trees can't talk.
Jack stood there, undecided, and then turned away from Deputy Bonnie. He ran smack in to a guy with ginger colored hair and a big smile. "Sorry bud," Jack told Detective Brenner and tried to walk around him.

"Sorry Jack," Detective Brenner replied and quickly placed a handcuff to Jack's left wrist, the closest one to him.

Jack stopped and gaped at him in complete surprise. "What the hell...," Jack said, starting to raise his right hand, curling the fingers into a fist and bringing it around towards Brenner.

"Whoa Jackie," said Deputy Thomas as she wrapped her hand around Jacks' right wrist. She stepped in behind Jack and Brenner applied light pressure to his handcuff to get Jack to turn away from both of them. Brenner handed the unattached cuff to Thomas who secured it on Jack's other wrist.

"Thanks Bonnie," Detective Brenner said.

"Anytime Detective," Deputy Thomas said smiling at Brenner. "Handsome, and what a nice body," she thought. He was always so pleasant when they had a chance to interact professionally. Tonight he seemed all business.

"What the hell, Bonnie," Jack said. He had just realized the predicament he was in and started to struggle a bit with the handcuffs.

"You are under arrest for the murder of Susan Miller," Detective Brenner said, and began reading the rest of Jack's Miranda Rights in front of Deputy Thomas as a witness.

"Murder," Jack screeched now, really struggling to get loose of his restraints. "Are you f-ing kidding, bud?"

Detective Brenner took one side and Deputy Thomas the other as they escorted Jack to Thomas' patrol car. Several other deputies were in the immediate area, keeping the other homeless and assorted lookers-on away from the arrest situation.

Jack yelled and cursed, struggling the whole way to the car. Once there, the law enforcement officers had to enlist the help of another deputy to get Jack safely in the car, without hurting himself or them. They buckled him into the secure plastic seat that prevented him from thrashing around.

"Jack, Jack....Jack!" Deputy Thomas said trying to get his attention. No luck.

"Hey officer, deputy, hey hey hey!" another homeless man shouted from the corner of Federal Highway and Lucerne Avenue. He was hopping up and down on one foot then the other. Detective Brenner walked towards the man.

"What's up, my friend," Detective Brenner asked. Another Palm Beach County Sheriff's Deputy moved in to assist.

"Hey, like Jack needs meds real bad ya know?" the man said speaking in rapid fire bursts. "He ain't right since that guy picked him up, and before that he ran out of his psych meds anyway. Or someone stole them." The man continued to hop from one foot to the other.

"Thanks guy, what's your name?" Brenner asked.

In response the man pivoted on one of his hopping feet and ran off down the sidewalk towards Brian Park.

Detective Brenner walked back to Deputy Thomas' patrol car. He joined the District Lieutenant there. "Can we get him to the hospital first, Lieutenant? Apparently he is on some psych meds that he stopped taking a day or so ago. We don't want a deputy to get hurt if he goes off."

Chapter Ten - Jack Goes To Jail

It felt good to know, one of the killers, was behind bars. Detective Brenner joined Dr. Ma and David, for a celebratory green juice, at the tiny fresh market north of Dr. Ma's home in West Palm Beach.

Ceelos Organic Produce Market, was a neighborhood gem. Fresh organic produce, specialty items like raw nut cheese, and granola, packed the shelves of the tiny store.

"Three Kale-a-bunga drinks," David ordered for them.

Detective Brenner put three raw organic cookies on the counter. "Add these to the tab. The cookies and the green stuff are on me," he said pulling out his credit card before Dr. Ma or David could object.

"Thanks again, docs," Detective Brenner said.

"Always, our pleasure, Jeremy," Dr. Ma replied.

"Pleasure?" David inquired. He was picking out a basket of organic, raw, vegetables to purchase. Fruit, too, the oranges looked great.

"At the result," Dr. Ma clarified. "Jeremy," she said. "We have a collaborator. Jack is not the only one responsible for Susan's murder."

"You have alluded to that, Dr. Ma, but where are you going with it?" Detective Brenner said.

"I don't know exactly yet," Dr. Ma replied, "but it is coming very soon."

"Well, you know I am ready, when you are," Detective Brenner said as he finished his cookie and reached for a second. "Are you going to eat that?" he asked Dr. Ma.

Ma shook her head in the negative. "No, go ahead, its good for you. We have to get back to work now, but I will get ahold of you as soon as we get on his trail."
"You know there is no evidence of anyone, other than Jack and Susan, at the crime scene," Brenner said.

"Not that you can see, Jeremy," Ma said, "not yet anyway."

David had dinner tonight at Karen's home in Palm Beach. He would leave after patient appointments, and Dr. Ma would take over the evening classes at the dojo. He had debated calling Karen after the first debacle, but something was different about the pretty young woman. He swore she *smelled* intriguing.

Dr. Ma and David left Detective Brenner browsing the specialty food items in the small front cooler, and arrived at the clinic, just after Winnie settled the first patients in the waiting rooms.

The day passed in a blur without either of them taking a proper lunch. Winnie had no such difficulty; she ate at her desk. The phone finally stopped ringing and the last patient, an emergency knee injury, hobbled in to see David.

"Hello, Dr. Anderson," the young yoga instructor greeted him as he walked in.

"Hello, Amy," David greeted her. "What is with the crutches?"

"I took a Yang Yoga class last week and then I stayed for the Yin class. When I got up at the end I felt a 'pop' in my knee."

"This led to crutches?" David prompted gently. "No," Amy said shaking her head. "It just got worse everyday and then I couldn't walk on it in a few days."

"Have you seen a conventional medical doctor?" David asked.

"No," she replied smiling a bit self consciously, "I wanted to come here first."

David sighed to himself. He was grateful for the trust his patients showed him and Dr. Ma, but sometimes he thought they went a bit over-board.

He examined her knee, and then said to her "I think you have a slightly misalignment of the meniscus. Dr. Ma and I can treat it or you can go to a conventional medical doctor. This is a somewhat significant injury."

"I would like you and Dr. Ma to treat it first," Amy said. "I already saw the attending doctors at school and their treatments haven't worked. They thought it was a sprain."

Amy was a first year medical student at the Traditional Chinese Medical School in Ft. Lauderdale. She had met Dr. Ma and David when they lectured at the school.

"Ok then," David said and went to get Dr. Ma.

"Do you have enough time, David?" Ma asked. She knew he had plans tonight, to see a young woman he met from the Save the Tiger events.

"I will, if I do the reduction, and you do the acupuncture followup," David replied hopefully.

"Of course," she answered. "Let's get to it."

Together they shifted the misaligned meniscus, and taped it to support healing. Dr. Ma set the needles for treatment ,and prepped a homeopathic injection for inflammation.

"Amy, I am sorry to leave you, but I have a prior engagement," David said taking her hand in his, and giving her a smile of encouragement. "Dr. Ma will finish up and then I want to see you tomorrow."

"No worries, Dr. Anderson," Amy replied. "I will see you tomorrow."
David said goodbye to Winnie, and left for home to get ready. He saw Jet, one of their student instructors, getting out of her car, as he finished tying his running shoes in the small lot behind the Zen garden.
"Bowing out on us tonight?" Jet asked smiling and giving him a respectful bob of her head.

David liked Jet, she was very dedicated to her training and would make a great instructor if she chose to continue with the dojo.

"In body, but not spirit, Jet," David replied. "Show Dr. Ma how well your form is coming along."

"Yes, Sifu," Jet replied, glowing a bit from his compliment.

David ran home to his little apartment behind Renato's Restaurant in Palm Beach. He loved the elegant old building, with curving stone steps up to a small landing and door on the second floor. The first floor was all tiny posh shops. The heady smell of Renato's kitchen followed him and reminded him he had skipped lunch.

David stopped at the reception area before he headed up. He didn't want to go to Karen's with his stomach growling. He didn't know what kind of food was going to be served. The Maitre d' saw him coming. "The usual?" he asked David.

"Please," David replied. "Just knock on the door." It was very convenient where he lived. Delivery was steps away. Renato's had his credit card on file. David's usual was a large bowl of barely steamed or raw vegetables lightly tossed with organic extra virgin olive oil, sea salt, and fresh spices.

David took the steps two at a time, and hurried to take a shower and dress. The food arrived, just as he wrapped himself in a towel, hot and steamy from the shower. He answered the door and signed the chit, adding a generous tip.

The young waiter hurried away without a word, happy to get a nice tip for a two minute delivery.

David practically wolfed his food down as he dressed. "Must not skip lunch," he thought, "bad for the digestion." Putting together a white silk crew neck t-shirt, navy Valentino v-neck cashmere sweater, and grey custom tailored wool slacks, he pulled on Manolo Blahnik loafers and headed downstairs. Karen had told him it would be casual cocktails, and a light dinner.

Karen lived with her parents in a lovely home, on the Intracoastal Waterway. It was just blocks from David's apartment, so he decided to walk. Their butler opened the door, and ushered him in to the library, where Karen and her parents were waiting, cocktails in hand.

David didn't drink alcohol, so he asked for a sparkling water. He hadn't expected to meet Karen's parents this evening. He recalled, that her father had mentioned doing business, with his father.

"Good to see you again, David," Karen's father boomed in his loud voice. He grasped David's hand in a semi-death grip. There was a somewhat surprised look on his face at the sheer, unmoving power of Davids hand.

David had lived in Palm Beach with his parents before they died. Their home was next to the McCarthy's. He never met Karen when he lived there. It seemed that Palm Beach kids often met in their late teens or 20's when they finished boarding school and sponged off of their parents. Before that they hardly saw each other in passing. School vacations were short and often spent traveling.

"My pleasure, Mr. McCarthy," David replied, careful not to return Karen's father's grip. He could easily crush the man's hand. Joseph McCarthy was a billionaire in electronics manufacturing. He was dressed neatly in a sport coat, polo shirt and slacks, that were put together for him at Ralph Lauren.

"Mrs. McCarthy," David turned to the delicate appearing older woman. She had that stretched, thin elegance of so many women in Palm Beach. Meticulously attired in a light green silk sheath and matching Gucci heels and bag, she had an ethereal air to her. David very carefully took her outstretched hand, and bowed slightly over it. Nobody kissed hands anymore.

"Well, we must be off," Ann McCarthy said in her soft Boston accent. She smiled at David knowingly. "You two enjoy. Perhaps I will see you at breakfast."
Taken off guard briefly by the insinuation, David blushed slightly. He was saved from answering her by Joseph who said loudly "I did some business with your father, David. Lets get together soon and play golf." David nodded at him. Before he could say more both the McCarthy's were out the front door and into their waiting car.

"Thank god," Karen said grabbing his arm, tugging him out of the library, and up the broad entranceway staircase. She was pulling him along as fast as she could get him to follow. At the first floor, she stepped left, off the sweep of marble stairs, and through a double carved door that stood open. A small, but well-appoint-

211

ed entry held a fireplace, club chairs, and a small table with food and drinks set out.

Karen closed the doors and turned to him smiling. She closed the space between them in moments and started kissing him while pulling at his clothing. The sweater was the first to go, and his shirt was partly untucked from his pants, by the time he managed to get a word out.

"So, no dinner?" David asked trying to slow her down. This was definitely not the speed at which things could happen for the tiger. His animal instincts were something he kept tucked away with human women.

"Oh there's something on the menu," Karen replied. "You."

David started to respond, when she reached over the table with the food and drinks and pulled off a pair of what appeared to be working police handcuffs. Startled, David stepped back as she moved forward dangling the cuffs and smiling.

"I am prepared, this time" Karen said opening one cuff, and reaching for his left wrist. "I didn't know you were into this."

David deftly avoided her, shadowing her movements, so she couldn't close the distance. "What possibly gave you that idea," he said keeping a careful eye on her, and staying just out of reach.

Karen stopped, frowning slightly. "That's what everyone says," she replied. "I couldn't figure out why you seemed so dangerous to me, the last time. I am ok with all that but," she trailed off, not finishing her sentence.
David angled away from her again. They seemed to be dancing around the small room. "Sorry, girl, but this is *definitely*, not my gig," he said.

One of the suite doors opened and a tall slim redheaded woman entered in a sheer top and even sheerer palazzo pants. "Am I late?" she smiled.

David stopped moving, regarding the newcomer with surprise. "What is going on?" he asked Karen, who had closed the gap between them, and was reaching again for his wrist with the handcuffs. The redhead came closer to them as well, and wrapped her cool, long fingered hand around his other wrist.

David pulled the handcuffs from Karen's grip and tossed them across the room. "This, ladies, is not happening. Honestly, I don't know what you have in mind, but I think its time for me to go."

"Incredible body," the redhead said as she stepped in front of him trying to block his exit.

David felt a slight shiver of fear. Pure animal instinct, he knew the two girls couldn't harm him, but any threatening movements could trigger his tiger instincts. "You two have been scammed," he said. "Someone gave you lousy information about me for tonight."

"Is that part of the game?" the redhead asked? "Denial?" Smiling, she wrapped her arms around his waist before he could back away.

"Ok, I'm in trouble if I don't leave right now," he thought. He couldn't separate the tiger from his human self completely. He always had to have very controlled encounters with humans to keep things safe. For everyone.
Karen stepped next to the red head and slipped one cuff on his wrist. He hadn't noticed her retrieving them. He felt a low growl start deep in his chest. He did the only thing he could do to keep from possibly harming them both. He ran.

David was fast and graceful. He easily slipped past the redhead after extracting his cuffed wrist from Karen. He snapped the one locked cuff with a powerful twist and dropped it on the staircase on his way down. Strength enough to break the cuff didn't mean it wouldn't leave a bruise. "Damn," he said as he registered the redness and small gash from where the stainless steel had given way.

Then he was out of the house and off the property before either woman could fully register he was gone from the room.

When she heard the front door slam, Karen grabbed her cell phone and tapped out a quick text message. She had his number stored in her contacts. His phone buzzed in his pocket, but he was too angry to look at it.

After several texts went unanswered, she tried calling him.

"David?" Karen said hesitantly when he answered. "I am so sorry, I thought this was what you wanted, and that's why the last time was a bust."

"Have you lost your mind?" he asked her, trying to control his tone. He was speaking softly as he walked towards his apartment.

"What man, wouldn't want two women all over him?" Karen said, defensively. She looked up as the redhead, Ena, left, closing the door to her suite. By the sheepish expression on Ena's face, Karen got the feeling she had been had. She shouldn't have confided in Ena, or the girls at the party what had happened, when she took David home with her the last time.

"So you haven't had this type of, um, thing, with some of the local girls?" she offered.

"What?" David said, his voice raising in anger. He stopped for a moment to calm down and speak softly. He didn't need someone calling the police department about a man shouting on his phone, walking the street.

This was Palm Beach. Some things were not acceptable. Many crazy things were accept-able, of course, but some things like shouting outside were most definitely not.
"What kind of crap is that? You invite me for dinner and your mother seems to think I will be there in the morning. Did she know you planned this?" David continued.

"No!" Karen said, her own voice raising a bit. "Well, maybe some of it," she realized how badly that sounded, even to her.

Despite his best efforts, David was just getting angrier. "So if *I* invited *you* for dinner and planned on some crazy sex thing without talking to you first or even knowing you more than a few hours, this would be ok with you?"

He took a deep breath. "Calm down, David," he thought. He turned onto Worth Avenue again and realized that he had been walking in a big circle.

"David, I am sorry," Karen said sounding upset "I just asked about you… the girls said you were into some crazy stuff… Ena offered to…" It was all coming out jumbled. She stopped and regrouped. "Ok that sounds lame, even to me."

"Look, Karen," David said interrupting her. "I have got to go, I have a long day tomorrow."

"I'll call you tomorrow," she started to say.

He interrupted. "No, just leave me alone." After a minute of silence, Karen hung up without answering him. David sighed, and slipped his cell phone into his pocket, after checking for work related messages.

Dr. Ma and David didn't believe in an answering service. After hours, the two forwarded the clinic lines, to their cell phones. Each one took alternating nights to answer incoming calls.

He didn't walk directly home after he spoke with Karen. He needed more time to calm down. He took a left on Peruvian and went over to the the docks. Large vessels full of luxury and high level technology, bobbed gently in the Intracoastal Waterway, south of the Okeechobee Bridge.

He stood on the seawall, looking out at the light traces from the vessel hulls, painting the water surface. A break in one, revealed the face of the Elder Sprite, from the other night.

He watched it silently for several minutes before she spoke to him. "I'm sorry, Great Cat, this is just your path, isn't it?" David understood the Sprite in his head. Their voices sounded like water lapping the hulls around him. Or someone talking into a tin can.

He forgot from the last time that Karen's suite windows opened onto the Intracoastal waterway. The Sprites had a ringside view of tonight's activities again. Humiliation twice in one week. He was probably setting a record. The Sprite disappeared below the water.

"Yes," David agreed with it grimly, it seems so. He pushed the memories floating at the edge of his consciousness away. Flashes of sensations, emotions, fear and anger. Memories of the first time he had lost control in an intimate encounter with a human.

"Never again," he promised himself. He didn't want to dredge up bad stuff. "Please go away," he pleaded silently with his memories. He recalled being reckless in battle after that first encounter went so wrong. Dr. Ma accused him of wanting to lose the precious life he had been given for this time around.

David and Dr. Ma were tough in battle with otherworldly bad guys, but, David still had a gentle soul when it came to humans. He couldn't bear the thought of harming in any way, a human when he was here to protect them. He may have been careless for a while. He had wracked up some impressive injuries, that was for sure.

Elementals cannot be killed in the manner otherworldly beings could. He could die in his human form, but it would take a lot. Living or not, he couldn't escape himself even if his human form died.

No matter what he was destined to suffer in this lifetime, he would just endure. There was no choice in the matter.

David turned towards home. He would see Dr. Ma in the morning and they would do what they were here for. They would solve Susan's murder, completely. He would never actually rest that night. His mind would be full of the past.

While David dealt with his evening, Dr. Ma had been talking to the birds in her backyard. Birds were her favorite form of messenger. Ma called on a Florida Mockingbird for this particular task. They had the greatest repertoire of mimicry, according to humans, but she knew they were actually multilingual.

She needed a bird, to help her pass a message, she knew would bring out the collaborator in Susan's murder. She knew who he was, but she still had to catch him. Most importantly, she wanted the Oni to come with him, unaware he was being set up. The police would deal with the human bad guy, and she would take out the non human. Literally. Like you took out garbage, to keep it from stinking up the house.

The little bird was a local resident. Mockers in Florida don't migrate. Sometimes their northern relatives came to warm up, but ours didn't leave. He knew just about everybody in the area.

"Take this message and have everyone spread it around," she told him. "I need the human and the Oni to both hear it, and more than once."

"Of course! Ma-sama," the little bird chirruped. "We will let you know what happens."

"ASAP," Dr. Ma emphasized. "I have to get this case finished."

The little bird nodded and flew off. She heard him muttering her directions to himself. "OCD," she thought, "but that works in my favor."

Chapter Eleven - The Garden

Dr. Ma was in the garden at her house, cutting those persistent lemon grass stalks for Alan at Ceebos Produce. She already had enough dried in her pantry to last a lifetime of teas.

She should really get David over here to dig the roots. That was the part of the lemongrass plant that was used for cooking. It was also strong enough for medicinal use.

When the Grackle landed next to her, and started telling her the result of last night's message system, she was elated. The collaborator had taken the bait she left. Time to call Detective Brenner with some new information about his other killer. The unknown conspirator would be revealed! The Oni was coming. *Show time!*

She turned to rise from her dirty knees, in the early morning light, and stopped, a strange vision coming over her. The Grackle's relation of events had drawn a thread of consciousness from the man she sought, directly to her. This wasn't current. It was not happening today, this vision. If she had to guess, it was when it all started, when the demon had gotten in.

She didn't know him, this man, but Susan had. Intimately. He had such evil in his heart. "Poor soul, to live like that," she thought. As the man contemplated his unhappy life, a dark shadow slipped behind him and waited.

Dr. Ma knew the presence waited for an opening. All the man had to do was conceive of an evil event and desire help to accomplish it. That was the opening, the darkness waited for, wanted.

The man closed his eyes and the shadow slipped closer. Suddenly the darkness, was sucked into the man sitting there in her vision. It was there one minute and gone the next.

"Ah!" Ma thought unhappily. "You let it in." The man's eyes opened in the vision, and he smiled. The solution he sought to his unhappiness, had come to him, literally.
"Evil was not a predator," Ma mused, "but an opportunist." Humans thought that evil hunted them, overwhelming and possessing them so they would commit horrible acts.

Not so.

Evil was like the baseball bat leaning against the wall of a dugout. Two players argued, one so angry he was practically homicidal. The other had recently slept with his fiance, effectively ending their engagement. As the angriest verbal combatant turned away he spied the innocent bat leaning against the wall.

In an instant, he grabbed the bat by the handle and with a practiced turn of the waist and shoulders, struck his rival in the head, killing him. Evil was just an opportunist. The bat hadn't jumped into the player's hands and forced him, to crack open his team mate's skull.

Dr. Ma had actually consulted on that case for Detective Brenner. It was nowhere near Brenner's jurisdiction. Another homicide cop had called him from Detroit. He had heard of Brenner's use of a local psychic.

The homicide cop was at a dead end in his investigation as to which player should have been the suspect. They knew it was someone on the team. Nobody had known about the affair. That, in itself, was amazing.
Dr. Ma, interrupted her musings, as she heard footsteps softly coming her way from the front yard walkway. The steps were so light, that nothing in her vicinity, heard them. Not the tiny wrens flitting in the bushes next to her, or the

stray cat she fed twice daily, who was stretched out in the sun in her plant trash pile.

David's passage was so silent, humans and animals wouldn't hear him unless he deliberately made noise. Which he did. Often. It saved the panic you would see when people (and pets) noticed him suddenly, standing closer than he should be, if you didn't hear him approach.

David walked through Dr. Ma's side garden gate. As the gate squeaked open, the cat bolted upright and fled into the nearest tree, to get a safe visual on the intruder. The little wrens fell completely silent, and still, to hide their positions. They would break for freedom, when they saw the direction he was going.

David saw her immediately, and walked towards her. When she hadn't answered her front door, he figured, correctly, that she would be in the garden. That was her peace and solace on her days off. Make things grow. Her garden grew, all right. Wild and crazy was a good description.

Anything you could think of to grow in the South Florida climate, you may find there. She collected and nurtured everything. David grabbed a ripe starfruit hanging from a set of twin trees, and bit into it as he walked towards her. Those trees seemed to always be putting out fruit. It definitely wasn't natural, but neither was Dr. Ma.

Ma was sitting very still next to that massive clump of lemongrass she couldn't keep in check. He recognized the signs of a recent vision in her stiff posture. She had garden tools all around her, and crumbling soil on her hands and knees. A neat pile of cut stems, lay to the side. The fragrance reached him in the early morning humid air.

Ma turned her head at his approach. He noted the messenger Grackle sitting on the bush next to the lemongrass. It flew off as he got nearer. "The Sprites saw the shadow that night," he said, commenting on the yet, un-broached topic. They knew each other, too well.

"I know," Ma replied. "You'll never guess who it is, either." She hadn't told him about all the information she got when the water Sprite linked her consciousness to Jack before his arrest. David didn't actually care about the details. He was a big picture kind of guy. Identify prey, hunt, and kill, were the points he followed in a plan. Why, he left up to her.

"Don't tell me, I love suspense," David said with unusual sarcasm.

Ma looked at him again. She noted he wore slightly rumpled clothing, probably, from the evening before. He had not changed yet. Not a good sign. She felt a sense of sadness emanating from him. Getting up in a swift and graceful move, she reached for him, gently embracing the tall, powerful man.

"Did you sleep in your clothes, child?" Dr. Ma asked softly. She knew he probably sat in Zazen (sitting meditation), all night. Elementals didn't truly sleep. She never did. She did try to rest her human body for eight to nine hours a night. When you had something important to process, sitting meditation worked just fine.

Like Dr. Ma, David would sit utterly still, and place his human body in the same type of restorative stasis by entering a deep delta state. To outside appearances, he was almost not breathing. Like her, his skin would be quite cool to the touch. Every time they demonstrated this state in class, the students would creep out when they went up to touch them briefly.

She knew, that something went wrong for David last night. He went to dinner with a young woman from the tiger charity event. David had confided that the first 'date' had ended poorly as usual. Last night was an attempt at a fresh start. "Young people rush their relationships," she thought. In David's case there were other factors at work. She, herself, understood the delicate nature of having an intimate relationship with a human.

Dr. Ma had endless compassion for David. He followed her on this path to help humans, every time trapping himself alone in the human world. "Lonely, gentle soul," she thought. "Tell me about it when you are ready," she said.

Painful emotion rippled across his features briefly as she looked at him. "When we have nothing better to discuss, perhaps," he said. "I thought it might be worth a shot."

She, herself, was alone. Her mate had passed beyond her reach here in this cycle of rebirth. At least she had his memory. David, her current tiger companion, never had a mate. The fact that she was no substitute for a proper mate to the vibrant young man, was not lost on her.

"I'm sorry, David." Ma turned back to gather her tools and plant trash. She didn't want to rub any fresh salt in the wound he was trying to hide from last night.

"Nothing to be concerned about, Ma-sama," David replied. His expression was a mask of composure. For the briefest moment he had allowed her to see his pain. He may never tell her how last night had gone. If he didn't share, she would not ask him, for further information.

The nearness of the dragon, when she hugged him, was intoxicating. They were meant for each other metaphorically. They were the yin and yang in an endless circle. Constant attraction and opposite natures fueled the circle's movement. Younger than her, he had a harder time with the balance. He was never sure if he wanted to rip her head or her clothes, off.

Shaking off his confusion, he said, "What is the plan?" Best to turn his energies to the task at hand.

Dr. Ma was always impressed by the resilient young tiger. "We will have to involve Brenner in this, again, to arrest the human, but I think we will need to get our hands on the Oni first, to keep everyone safe."

"Same drill?" David asked. He looked away from her, still feeling the residual sensation of her holding and comforting him. They would never be together, she and he.

Hearing the lower tone in his voice and knowing what what going on, she regretted her embrace of him. They usually didn't touch, knowing both would feel that inevitable tug. She reminded herself to focus on the job ahead. Her mate had been a powerful tiger, and their intimacy had been explosive.

"Same drill," Dr. Ma confirmed. Those two words, *same drill*, was the description of how, they took on otherworldly foes. Their specialties depended on who fought, and who held balance.

David, speaking the two words first today, meant that he would handle the outside environment, and she would handle the removal of the Oni from the man it had used as a receptacle. Removal of the demon was necessary, so the police could safely arrest the human.

This balancing act, between the two of them, was a thousand years old. The humans, and the otherworldly foes, changed faces. The earth's geography, changed in subtle ways. The world rulers, and societies, changed in dramatic ways, but, their job never changed.

The fun, and the danger, came from never knowing exactly what you were dealing with. Quick thinking, and subtle environmental changes, may be needed to accomplish their part, without revealing the true nature of the be-ing who orchestrated the murder.

Dr. Ma caught David up, on everything the bird spies, had found out for her.

It was time to hunt.

Chapter Twelve - The Plan

How do you turn the tables, on a stone cold murderer? Someone who could arrange his wife's gruesome murder, and play the grieving spouse, without a hitch?

Someone who concealed a demon inside him, that was pulling the strings? Ok, not completely fair in that assessment of string pulling. You have to have the strings to pull. You have to have a heaping casserole of depravity and a side of evil intentions to tempt the demon, over for dinner.

Ma and David disliked Oni. Actually, who didn't dislike Oni, other than Oni.
They smelled so strongly to otherworldly creatures, it almost seemed like you could taste the way they smelled. Dr. Ma and David had tasted that distinctly foul smell at the murder scene, in Palm Beach.

Oni were also referred to as yokai. They seemed to have arisen from the mountains of Japan. Dr. Ma assumed that coming from the bowels of the earth under the mountains gave them a disgusting, decayed odor.

To be fair, it could have been their actual composition of mountain dirt and muck. Dr. Ma had been very surprised to find the evidence of one such creature at the murder scene. Florida, was a bit out of its habitat. Allen Miller, must have picked it up in his travels. This type of creature, was often bound, to location of origin.

David had complained that he couldn't get the stench out of his sensitive tiger nostrils, for days.

Dr. Ma was luckier. Dragons had selective scent capability. If it wasn't of interest to her, she just didn't smell it. She thought that David was slightly exaggerating. There was an old tiger vendetta over Oni wearing tiger skin loincloths.

"Obviously, the skin came from a dead tiger," David had expressed to her hotly. "A garment that was no longer attached, to the tiger it came from." He would have gladly switched places with her dispatching this demon. Balance dictated, that the air Element, her, dispatched the earth element demon.

The next time they encountered an air element demon, David would be up to bat. Water and

Fire element demons, were a toss up. Dr. Ma
and David, had equal strengths in both areas.

Dr. Ma showered and changed, after confirming
with Detective Brenner, he could convene a
task force to arrest Allen Miller tonight. He
asked her for a brief outline of information. The
rest would come later, when he was able to
gather physical evidence and a confession.

In Detective Brenner's office with undercover
and tactical officers from Palm Beach, and the
Palm Beach County Sheriff's office, they had
put together an operational plan.

The human bait had been put out prior when
Dr. Ma connected to Jack's consciousness. The
information, had given her a method of finding
him.

Undercover sources had spread the word that
law enforcement was looking for a friend of
Jack's, after his arrest. They were looking for a
homeless man, who was in possession of evidence from the murder, that had not been located when Jack was arrested.
They even hinted, that they were close to finding the man, in the Lake Worth area. What Dr.
Ma knew after her chat with the Mockingbird,

was that the Oni, and his human, had taken the bait.

Tonight, Allen Miller would go looking for Jack's belongings. Things that may tie Miller to the murder. A note and a souvenir. Left with Jack's friend. All lies of course to lure him. Them.

Truthfully, they had confiscated Jack's belongings, after his arrest. Except something that his friend who told them about Jack's need of medication, might have taken or kept as his own. Always use a grain of truth.

Jack's friend had come to them complaining, that he had nothing belonging to Jack. "Why had they told everyone I did?" he asked.They put him in protective custody, and 'borrowed' his clothing and camp site for the operation.

This was not because any of the law enforcement officers knew about the human/Oni combination that would come looking for the friend. None of them knew about that, even Detective Brenner.
No, they were more worried that some wacko, that arranged for a mentally ill homeless man to brutally kill his wife, might be willing to off another homeless guy who could burn him.

To make sure Allen didn't change his mind, they had the friend write a note this morning and drop it off at Allen's home. It was left right on the front stoop, under a carefully placed rock, so it wouldn't blow away.

The security cameras covering Allen Miller's front door, showed the homeless man, (not his face) leaving the note. The cops had him tip his head down so the brim of his cap would obscure his facial features.

An undercover cop, similar to the homeless man's build, wore the pants and coat of Jack's friend. Only the outer clothing of course. Bad enough. He had his own underwear, socks, long sleeve t-shirt and BDU pants under the dirty outer garments. The shoes were his, covered in dirt and dried mud. The smell of the pants and coat, borrowed from Jacks old camp friend was, well, ripe.

The UC cop was sure, he would need more than one hot shower, to scrub out that smell. The cop sat, half in shadow, dressed in the homeless guy's clothes. He was in full view for when Allen started towards the camp. A streetlight above the area would make sure he was seen.

There were also a few personal items of Jack Daniels Kelly's to give authenticity to the made up homeless character's claims that he had something incriminating from Jacks' left behind belongings. A 'VOTE OBAMA' button pinned to the outer coat and a green plastic lei from St. Patricks day around his neck set the stage. Allen should recognize those, they thought.

10-97 (the code for someone's arrival, in this case, Allen) quietly buzzed in everyone's ear-pieces. All of the law enforcement officer's ear pieces. Dr. Ma and David were not part of the operation. They weren't even supposed to be there. Officially. Brenner knew they were around the back and south side of the now un-der construction Waterview Hotel.

The officers officially on the Op were staggered in a loose perimeter around Brian Park proper and Lake Avenue's east end. There was a small homeless population living among the sparse trees by the waterfront. Even smaller tonight, as every one of them had been replaced by an undercover officer.

The real homeless from the small camp were enjoying a hot meal a few blocks away in the church on the north side of Lucerne Avenue. The room was where they held yoga classes on

Tuesday and Thursday every week. The space held the men and women from the Brian Park camp nicely while the officers tried to catch the killer.

Their suspect, Allen Miller, was a tall white male in a dark windbreaker with the hood pulled up over his head. He approached quickly and quietly, looking around as he came. His hands were shoved deeply into his pockets.

One hand was twisting the note he received, or so he thought, from the homeless man who had Jack's possessions. "The man who was trying to blackmail him! Him!" he thought, furiously. This scummy asshole would regret ever having heard of him when he was done tonight.

Twisting the note into a small, sweat soaked ball only increased his anxiety and rage. Allen Miller was a desperate man. He had to get anything left behind by Jack when he was arrested.

Everything had gone as planned until now. He was a prepared kind of guy. It was, after all, his wife's murder. Detail and preparation had been his focus for months now.

Yes, Allen had everything planned out. He believed himself to be smart, cunning, and above all, able to get away with murder. After all, Susan had outlived her usefulness. Time to go my dear, he had thought. I need to move on from here.

They met in college, he and Susan. She had been track and field and he was on the swim team. Busy athletes at the top of their game. They dated between games and workouts and exams and, they never got to know each other well, did they?

She was a 100 meter standout. A knee injury had pushed her into cycling after graduation, instead of staying with running as a sport. Top athlete that she was, she had soon excelled in cycling. She joined a club, then a team and began to compete regularly.

He had been a 100 yard freestyle swimmer in the individual events. He tried the 200 yard relay, but it seemed he didn't play well with others. His talent, kept him from being booted off the team. He quit prior to graduation.

Allen told everyone a chronic ear infection, had sidelined his competitive swimming career. It was really, his self-absorbed personality. Nobody from the swim team contradicted his version. They were glad to be rid of him. Everyone felt, there was something inherently wrong, with the man. There was.

This is what would attract the Oni demon to him. That inherent wrongness and his desire to do bad things. Really bad things.

He was a physics major and she psychology. Both were at the College of Arts and Sciences, Cornell University. It was convenient. They graduated the same year and started their respective careers. Until Allen met the shadow being. He was attending a physics seminar in Japan. He went solo, but came back attached. Sometimes your hopes and dreams do come true. Allen's dreams of personal gain and professional domination, had always seemed just out of reach. Until the demon, came into his life.

Trying to excel at everything, Allen, worked out in his gym daily. He trained until he was exhausted, almost delirious. He wanted to test his physical limitations. How far could he go, before failure.

Stopping when his muscles began to shake and refuse to respond to his commands, he would wrap himself in a large old terry cloth robe, complete with a hood to absorb his sweat, and keep the chill away. Then he would sit silent, in a type of meditation. It was more of a, *focus your energies* session, really.

Allen would sit and recover himself after the brutally hard workout. When he could focus on a single thought, that thought would be, *succeed*. Obsessively repeated, he meant *success at any cost. Success in any way.*
Allen always felt inferior. He didn't know why. His wealthy, educated parents doted on him. He had everything that money could buy. Nannies, cooks, playmates, and so on. He could do no wrong, in his parents opinion.

Even if he killed someone, he used to think. Funny how things manifest themselves from our private minds to our waking lives. Susan, his wife, had been his first kill. A necessary sacrifice, of course. He couldn't stay close to someone, be smothered by someone, and be responsible to someone, if he was going to rule the world! "Rulers were solitary in essence. They had companions at will," he would tell himself

Allen often succeeded well above his competitors, but that didn't matter. He wanted to always be ahead by miles, not inches. Best wasn't enough.

Susan had fit into his long term plan, until recently. She was pretty, educated, well spoken, and from a wealthy family. Her father had been a car parts magnate. He sold the business and retired at 50 years old. Two years later, he was dead of a heart attack.

Susan and her mother, had been left very well off. That was part of the plan. Allen had money of his own from his family. He stood to inherit the whole caboodle, when his parents kicked it. Until then, he had Susan's money. Susan's family money when her mother was gone.

He was never going to make a boatload of money in his own career. Just professional successes came his way. Bullshit plaques and awards. A University job such as he had was about top of the line in expectations unless you were a notable brainiac. That type of physicist got paid by companies and other private interests.

Allen, was a physics teacher at the local university, Palm Beach Coastal College. He was part of the Intellectual Foundation Program. "Hard to tell by the name," he would think, "when you met some of the idiot students getting funds from it."

After he absorbed the power of the shadow, he now considered everyone an idiot, not just students.

One day at the seminar in Japan, sitting in meditation and focused on gaining power and dominion over everything, he felt something. Something tapped on his shoulder so to speak. An opportunity knocking.

It wasn't a voice or a tangible presence. It was a feeling. So strong this thing was. It was just outside of him, asking to come in and help him with his desires.

All he had to do, was open himself to the opportunity. Let it in, to help him succeed with his plans. It was like finding a winning Lotto ticket on the sidewalk. You could pick it up, or leave it there. You would pick it up if you were smart. You would tuck it into your pocket, if you were cunning.

Allen remembered smiling, when he realized the purpose of the presence lurking just outside him. Waiting. Wanting to help. Finally! Right there. He imagined himself open to the waiting darkness and in it slithered. Smooth as silk.

He noticed nothing physical at first, after he returned home to the USA. Well, maybe a boost in confidence. Maybe a feeling of power, that made him laugh out loud while sitting in his meditations, sweaty hooded robe wrapped around him for warmth.

Later, much later, he felt the benefit of letting in the shadow. So many things fell into place. More powerful every day, he was able to speak his truth to all idiots, without censure. He was able to do what he wanted, without restriction. Except for Susan. Susan didn't buy into the new Allen.

Allen decided Susan was in the way of his ultimate success. She didn't understand the new power the shadow had bestowed upon him. She didn't understand his master plan!

Susan was always complaining these days. She said he wasn't the man she met. No shit, he wasn't! He was a much greater man. He was enhanced with the addition of the dark presence.

At first, he just fantasized about killing Susan. Each time he got rid of her, life was so much better. As he completed the fantasy each time, each day, he began to add details. Details of how, when, and where, details of whom.

Oh yes, there was a who, to do the deed. He, Allen, was the puppeteer, the great master of the ultimate design. Someone like him didn't do the dirty work. There were people for that. People to get their hands dirty with death. Susan's death.

Allen would see the homeless men and women gathered, in the Lake Worth Town Square, everyday when he came to work at his building on Lake Avenue.

His office was in the newly built professional suites of the Waterview Tower on Lake Avenue.

"Man," he had thought. It had taken years to get those *amateurs* on the Lake Worth City Council to let the developer get going in real time on the Waterview Hotel renovation. He, Allen, would have moved faster. The results were spectacular. Hotel, club, restaurant and commercial office space.

Allen was a research physicist. He wasn't staff at Palm Beach Coastal College. He was adjunct. After he accepted the power of the shadow, however, his research seemed to dry up and the college was calling him with less and less frequently to teach.

He took the small commercial office space in the Waterview, to get out of the house, and away from Susan. They got on each other's nerves, in close quarters.

Susan had a small private practice, with an office in downtown West Palm Beach. Allen didn't know how she stood all the hustle and bustle of the City of West Palm Beach during the day. Her office was on Clematis Street in an old renovated building. The parking was atrocious, so she rode her bike to work more often than not. It was Florida after all, good weather all year round.

All this riding and training made her predictable. Being predictable made her an easy target, to plan to kill. He called her, when the GPS on her iPhone, showed her crossing the Southern Boulevard bridge. You have to love those safety features like real time tracking when she rode alone.

He knew her well enough, to anticipate she would stop to answer him, on the east side of the bridge at the little parking area. Jack had been strategically placed on the apex of the south side of the bridge.

The call from his office phone to his wife out cycling, was a great alibi for Allen. How could he have been involved in any way if he was nowhere near the site of her murder? All he had to do, was delay her long enough for Jack to reach her by foot, and get ready to approach.

Allen had timed Jack several times in preparation while sitting in his car in the north side parking area. Three minutes to the base of the bridge. Two more fiddling with his little cart, and then Jack would approach anyone in the area for a handout.

Money, food, a cigarette butt, it was all good. You see, Allen hadn't picked Jack randomly. The Oni demon had noticed Jack in the area more than once, and had prompted Allen to study him as a potential collaborator. Demons were great judges of character. Potential evil character, of course.

After watching and timing and plotting, Allen had followed Jack to his Brian park location. It was a good seven miles south or so. Quite a long haul for the homeless man, Allen had thought. Must be good pickings along the route and back, to prompt that long a walk.

It was a whole day's undertaking though, Jack's walk. Allen had to fudge a bit to spend the day tracking the homeless man for his murder prep.

Wouldn't want Susan to get a hint he was doing something out of the ordinary. Not that she checked up on him during the day. Allen was just a bit OCD, and didn't like to leave any details dangling to trip him up, if there was an investigation.

It was boring as hell, following Jack all day. If not for the persistent presence of the Oni, talking to him, encouraging him that this was the solution to his problem, he may have lost interest and looked for another helper.

Another helper may not have been as successful as Jack had been. Overall, with the help of his in house demon, Allen had planned and executed a nice and tidy murder. Until now.

Chapter Thirteen - Show Time

As Allen Miller turned south off of Lake Avenue and walked the hidden path behind the new Waterview Hotel, the perimeter officers held their positions. There was nowhere he could go, except up a high concrete wall. The path, began on Lake Avenue, and came out of the south side, of the new hotel.The side facing Brian Park.

There were officers on the perimeter with perfect views of all aspects. Just not the path itself. An undercover there, would be a dead give away. The private property was guarded, monitored by surveillance, and needed a key card to enter and leave the path through high metal gates.

Allen Miller had such a key card. His office was the tall concrete building to the west of the hotel. The path ran neatly between the two buildings. It curved between a lushly landscaped area with trees, bushes, waterfalls, and fresh mulch. Dr. Ma and David were waiting there by a cooperative tree. It was the perfect ambush, for the Oni demon.

They heard the metal gate clang closed. They both transformed seamlessly. The dragon and the tiger were now waiting. *Show time.*

The tiger opened a massive mouth and roared. Silently. To human ears. The otherworldly beings heard it. For miles. The vibrations of his roar slowed everything down. The quick staccato of steps from Allen Miller, had come to a complete stop midway along the path. The human couldn't move. The Oni demon could, if it left its human host's body. It left.

The dragon struck first. As the demon pulled free from the top of Allen Millers head the dragon was on it. Reaching behind, the demon pulled a flaming sword out of mid air and swept downward. David reached the human, before he could be cut in half by the demon's sword. Killing your recent host, was a common theme, among such demons.

Swatting Allen aside with his paw, the tiger roared again, directly in front of the demon. Allen rolled from the tiger's blow and came to a stop, against the back of a waterfall, dazed. The second the Oni hesitated, was enough for the dragon. Leaping into the air she grasped it, with her powerful back claws, and launched them both upward.

The tiger, watched them disappear, up and up before transforming into his human guise. Dressed in black, he picked Allen up and asked him "Are you okay Mr. Miller?" Taken aback by the use of his name, Allen hesitated before answering. David said, "Joe from Security sir. Don't you remember me?"

Allen Miller was too important to remember any security guard but he was trying to process what just happened. "What the hell is going on here, *Joe*?"

"I'm sorry, Mr. Miller, some kids jumped the gate and tried to mug you. I think. I got here, just after they knocked you down. If you are okay, I want to call the police."

"No!" Allen almost shouted. He got ahold of himself, and thinking fast, said,"No you idiot, we don't need the police to think our security is crap here. Go back to your post and watch the cameras. That's all you're good for."

The last thing Allen needed, were cops everywhere, to muck up his rousting of Jack Daniels' homeless buddy.

Allen brushed himself off, and walked towards the east gate, and Brian Park. "Good luck,"

David thought and smiled, "you asshole. Going to jail tonight, you are. Serves you right."

Allen, was feeling oddly alone, as he exited the south gate. Something happened, and he couldn't put a finger on it. Must have hit my head back there. He saw the homeless man in front of him, wearing dirty clothes. He looked a lot like Jack Daniels. They all looked alike. The 'VOTE OBAMA' pin and stupid green plastic lei, were in full view

"Figures, the stupid, and probably drunk, guy, voted for Obama," Allen thought. He forgot all about the incident on the path. He hurried forward to confront the dirty vagrant.
"I got your note," Miller said angrily, bearing down on the man. "You think you can fuck with me, buddy?" Miller pulled a small handgun from his jacket pocket. It hadn't fallen out on the path, because he had the holster sewn in, to facilitate concealed carry. Not that he needed a firearm. Until tonight.

The homeless man mumbled something, and turned away towards the park. "Hey" Miller said leveling the firearm. "I will shoot you where you stand, you dick."

"Police! Drop the weapon!" came the strident cry of voices all around him. Miller hesitated. The situation wasn't sinking in. "Police! Drop the weapon! Do it now. Drop the weapon! Do it now! Police! The orders kept being repeated. The officers surrounding him knew, that people get tunnel vision in stressful situations. Repeating simple commands, can get them to comply, eventually.

Allen, focused on the man, in front of him. "He was gone! When had he run away," Allen thought. "I was distracted by the police. He ran when they started yelling at him, Allen."

Allen turned to the voices coming from behind him. His hands in the air, he slowly knelt down and put his little Glock 27 on the ground. "I was being attacked by that homeless man officers," he said loudly. "This is all a mistake."

Suddenly the homeless man came back into view in front of him. Allen pointed wildly. "There he is," he shouted. "He was trying to rob me. I am a business man at the Waterview complex. Ask Joe, the security guy."

The homeless man was taking off his ball cap, pants, and bulky coat. Underneath was a clean cut young cop, in BDU's. Tactical vest and weapons made it clear, he was not who Allen had thought he was. The cop came forward, and stepping behind Allen he cuffed his hands, pulling him to his feet by his upper arm.

"I, I," Allen started.

"I," the cop said, "would keep my mouth closed if I were you. You have the right to remain silent," the cop began.

Allen listened in shock to his rights being read to him the short walk back to the patrol car. "How could this happen to him? Him!" Suddenly he knew what he felt was wrong. Something was missing. *IT* was missing! "Noooooo!" he screamed into the air.

Many miles above, the dragon dropped the Oni demon. It was very cold in the high altitude they had achieved. The flames on the demon's sword were out. The earth born creature was shivering, and stiff. The dragon chuckled. "Fly little demon, you don't want to fall from this height."

The Oni glared at her with hatred, trying to un-fold its wings in the cold. Stiff, they barely opened. Cold, they barely beat. It began to fall.

Earth born creatures didn't belong in the upper atmosphere. It cursed at the dragon.

"I'm sorry," the dragon said. "I didn't catch that, through your chattering teeth. Warm you up a bit?" Flames enveloped the demon from the dragon's breath. Heat did a demon good. It's wings flapped more rapidly holding it aloft. Reaching behind, it pulled another flaming sword from apparently thin air and charged at the dragon.

"That's the spirit!" the dragon said. As the Oni closed the gap between them, brandishing its' sword with a scream. The dragon exhaled again. Ice crystals formed over the smelly creature, freezing it mid stroke as it aimed the sword, for her neck.

"Didn't know about that little trick now, did you?" Air Elementals controlled fire and ice. It was likely the Oni had never met one. At this moment, it certainly never would, again. The dragon turned away and swatted the frozen demon with its powerful tail.

Demon ice shards scattered, like fractured diamonds, across the frozen night sky.

"Might have a brief rain shower by the time those reach the ground," the dragon said, pointing her nose towards the lights along the Intracoastal. "Or, just more humidity."

David was waiting for Dr. Ma, in the median of the Lake Worth bridge, when she walked up. She had landed on the rooftop of the new hotel, and transformed. A quick elevator ride to the ground floor, and she walked out into the humid night after the officers from the Op were all dispersed.

The well fed homeless, were making their way back to camp. None gave her a second look. She wasn't very clear to human eyes unless she chose to be.

David grinned as she walked up. "May I interest you in a late night dinner from Renato's?" He had ordered earlier, and asked the Maitre d', to have it ready by about 10:00 PM. They would pick it up, when Dr. Ma drove David back to his apartment.

"Pasta?" she said. "Of course! I'm starving." They walked over to her Mercedes, parked by the golf course fence, and got in. "David?" she said.

"Yes?" David answered, looking at her in the light from the golf course perimeter lamps.

"Great job," She smiled at him and leaned over to kiss him lightly on the cheek.

David's heart stopped beating for a second. "Thanks, you too Ma-sama."

They drove off, as the cops were still breaking up their operation. The fun part was over. The hours of cleanup, debriefing and paperwork were still ahead.

For Detective Brenner, it may mean an all nighter. Coordinating with more than one juris-diction was beyond time consuming, when you were the one who had asked for help.

Everyone involved, needed justification, for the expenditure of tax payer dollars. He had pa-perwork that would go on and on. Then there was the face to face thank you's, and hand shaking that was obligatory.

Brenner really did end up working all night. His office was covered in boxes and files, but a phone call early the next morning was the jack-pot.

He was happy that Allen Miller had been caught tonight. Best was that the guy was telling everyone who would listen, every detail of the crime His distraught attorney could do little, to stop him. No doubt an insanity defense would be on the table for him. You have to love these wackos with huge egos. Getting caught, frustrated them so much, they just told it over and over.

"Also too bad," Brenner thought, Jack Daniels, that crazy homeless guy the murder victim's husband employed to kill his young wife, had regained his memory. Not the memory of killing her. Just the memory of Allen Miller hiring him to kill her.

Regained it in detail, once he was back in the hospital on his meds. "Sucks to be you Allen," Brenner smiled.

Jack Daniels testimony, would put the final nail in Allen Millers' coffin now, that the psychiatrist could verify his sanity. Had to be considered sane, or close, for the courts to allow him to testify.

The poor man was distraught, over being charged with killing Susan Miller. The shrink believed that he had no real memory of the incident. He just believed what they told him he had done, to her. Jack was still going to be convicted of the murder, and would remain in jail a long long time. All he avoided with his confession, was the death penalty.

"Funny thing," the shrink had said. "Jack was sure he deserved everything he got, in his murder trial. He said he wouldn't even have contested the death penalty if he got it. After all, he had killed her hadn't he?" Ol' Jack believed that he was as responsible for her death, as her husband, Allen Miller.

"I am the killer," Jack kept repeating, but he hadn't been able to pull up details of the killing in his memory. Oh, had he tried. He wanted to make sense of the crazy thoughts in his head every night when he fell asleep.

Such strange dreams every night. He wasn't the killer in those dreams. He watched a young woman in those dreams, stopping to talk to a homeless man, and getting punched in the face for her trouble.

He watched her fall, in the dream every night. Fall, with her bike tumbling on top of her. Then, she would get dragged back, off the side of the road, onto Bingham Island. He told the psychiatrist all this. He said he could see it, but he wasn't the guy doing it. Someone, or some-*thing,* was dragging or *flying* with her, to a little area south of where she was punched.

It wasn't Allen Miller either, in the nightmarish dream. It was what looked like a homeless guy. Dressed like him. Only he had no face, just a dark mask.

The guy would get to that area further south, and put the woman's body on the ground there, face up. Picking up a chunk of concrete he brought with him, in his right hand, he smashed the woman's face. Jack always started scream-ing in his dream, about then. The prison guards would hear him and see him thrashing around in bed.

The dream would just go on. The young woman lying on the ground, had just begun to moan, and maybe wake up. The concrete was from the roadside where he first punched her. No, not him, the shadow faced, homeless guy!

The concrete piece looked like something that fell off a construction truck. Detective Brenner had recovered that concrete from the crime scene. It was covered in Susan's blood, bits of bone and teeth fragments were still stuck to it.

"Smack," Jack would hear as the homeless man, with no face, smashed her mouth again. The forceful second blow was breaking the lower jaw and more teeth. This was when Jack would start to cry, and wish he could block out what he saw.The guy that wasn't him, reached into the opening, that used to be her mouth. He grabbed a handful of the tooth and bone debris, and pitched it into the dark water of the Intra-coastal waterway.

"Stop, stop!" Jack always started to say when he got to the last part of his now nightmare. Shadow face, homeless guy, took out a utility knife. He roughly cut off the pads of her fingers. Jack couldn't understand why anyone would do that. "He just cuts her fingers, like that," Jack would say, crying. The prison guards and other inmates heard this too. Every night.

These bloody tidbits were dropped, left for the crabs and small birds, that would find them, next to the body and take them away for food.

Jack just knew it wasn't him. Couldn't be him! He was sickened by the dream. He begged for something to take the dreams away. Something to bring back sleep.

He told the psychiatrist he could never do such a thing, but she hadn't believed him. Dr. Stock was a kindly appearing, older woman, but she hadn't shown compassion for old Jack. No sir, she didn't.

The doctor kept telling him he was 'hiding the truth from himself' about why he did it. She was wrong! It wasn't him. "It was the shadow home-less guy," Jack would tell her. "Maybe it looked like him, Jack, because the guy possessed him or something." Dr. Stock didn't buy that either.

Jack just kept dreaming, waking up the other inmates every night. The prison put him in soli-tary to keep them from killing him to get some rest.

Chapter Fourteen - Detective Brenner Closes A Case

When a case takes an unexpected turn, it dredges up old feelings. Detective Jeremy Brenner loved solving a murder, for the victim. For their loved ones and friends.

When the case was closed, he would have time to reflect. Time to feel sorry for the victim. For their family and friends. For the cops and crime scene techs, the prosecutors, judges and juries, who relived the details in court. All those strangers who were more intimate with the victim in death, than they ever would have been with her, in life.

There was something soul baring, about a murder case. One of the most important times of your life, your death, will be laid out for everyone. Pictures, lab reports, models and charts, will give away all your secrets. There is nothing that won't be known, by the time the case goes to trial.

Detective Brenner, sat at his desk in the Palm Beach Police station, staring out of the window, at the displays in the store across from the split roadway.

There was the northbound County Road on the station side, and the southbound County Road, on the other side of the fountain. Recent renovation had restored the weathered fountain, and a fenced sitting area with grass had been installed, on each side. Jeremy loved the peaceful, landscaped break in the constant north and south bound traffic.

The unit secretary stuck her head in the door. "Pizza?" she said smiling. It was pizza Thursday. The lieutenant bought a few greasy pies from that place that delivered nationally. The one whose CEO sponsored lots of football ads.

"Sure," he responded. She left, knowing he would never make it to the break room, today. He knew it too. Processing day was for thinking, alone, in Brenner's book. Mulling over the details, to make sure you had new tools for the next one.

There was always going to be a next one.
He turned his attention out of the window again. His office window, was on the second floor. The store windows he was staring at, were on the first floor. He looked down into them and their displays of bright clothing.
Brenner like the cheerful Lily prints. Mrs. Pulitzer had been a resident of the island for

many years. Her house had been beautifully decorated, he thought, under the cats, birds, and clutter of a lifetime.

The large number of cats she cared for had left a certain, *ambiance*, to the house and grounds. Her family sold the place after she died, auctioning the contents.

Brenner had taken flack from the guys in the department for wearing his Lily ties at work. He finally left them for after hours events.

A defense attorney he knew in West Palm Beach had a thing for Disney. His Mickey Mouse ties were thought by some, not Brenner, to be the reason he wasn't nominated for a local judgeship. "Pity," Brenner thought. "Any man willing to wear Disney ties in criminal defense must be pretty self-confident. Or, a bit crazy. Same thing, when it came to a good defense attorney."

Brenner was glad to put this case to rest. A homicide in Palm Beach proper. What was the world coming to? Low life murder on the island. Not even a socialite murder situation.
Well, with Dr. Ma and David's help they had solved what would likely have become a cold case in no time. Odd discrepancies, and a lack

of evidence apparent from the start, would have stopped the case in its tracks.

Brenner didn't know everything, Dr. Ma and David were capable of, or how in fact they got some of their information, but he was grateful. Susan Miller deserved justice. Her killer, her piece of crap husband Allen, deserved to rot in hell.

Unfortunately, he would get a jail cell. If he ever got out of the funny farm. High security psych hospital for now. Little or no freedom of movement outside your room, but you had three hots and a cot. You also got television, free college education, and the companionship of your shrink, and the guards. Brenner had some less liberal ideas, of what such a prisoner should get, or not get.

At least the judge hadn't bought the insanity defense garbage, completely. Not all of it. Detective Brenner would have been furious, if the murdering bastard, got a cozy gig in some mental facility and then got out in a few years. That would have been a slap in the victim's face.

Allen Miller had a good lawyer. The guy had avoided an official 'nut job' title with his conviction. Temporary insanity. "I was crazy then. I'm not now. Go easy on me judge," he had said at his sentencing

"What a crock," is what Brenner thought.

This defense spared Allen the death penalty. In all honesty, Brenner couldn't disagree with Miller being a nut job after hearing the guy go on about being possessed by an evil entity and all that bunch of crap.

Dr. Ma and David, were very interested in that part of Allen Miller's confession. They asked Jeremy for an unofficial transcript, of just that section. Seemingly never to be surprised by anything, it was if they *expected* the information he was giving up.

Brenner had his own opinion, on whether crazy, meant no death penalty. "Of course, you were f —-ing crazy, if you killed your wife." Or had someone else do it. Who would consider that the act of a sane man? No one.
The law said, that crazy people, couldn't be killed for their crimes. "Lousy," Brenner thought. "Kill them like they killed their victims. Zero tax dollars going to feed and house you after that, you shits."

Brenner kept his thoughts to himself, in this time of bleeding heart liberals. It wasn't good for career advancement. Besides, who cares what he thought?

He closed his official case file, and re-taped the evidence bags he was holding onto, to finish the case. Walking all of them down to the Records and then Evidence Divisions, he dropped them off.

"You can rest now Susan," he thought. "We got them both." Later today, Brenner would buy a fresh bouquet of flowers, and place them on her grave site. She wasn't there yet. The Medical Examiner's office had to sign, stamp, and exe-cute, a short novel of paperwork to release her to her family for burial. Family that wasn't Allen Miller.

She had a plot though. Her grave had been dug and was ready now, to receive her, when they dropped her off at the funeral home. Hopefully later today. That way she may see the flowers he left next to the gaping wound in the earth.

The guys at the funeral home were good to him. They would put the flowers on the fresh dirt they mounded up over her coffin when they were done. Her headstone was weeks away.

The family didn't know what to engrave on the stone now. Susan's husband's name was no longer going to grace her inscription.

Miserable bastard.

Detective Brenner walked out the front door after dropping everything off. It was a beautiful day. He was going to walk over to Starbucks Coffee in the Esplanade and enjoy some of it. He certainly had worked hard enough these past weeks. A caramel macchiato would do the trick.

Chapter Fifteen - David And Joseph

Dredging up memories and feelings, is what tragedy does best. Humans being what they are, bringing up feelings, is less popular than covering them up. Alcohol, sugar, sex, shopping, they all worked. Pick a combination of whatever you liked.

David set up a golf game with Joseph McCarthy, on his day off, because the man would not stop calling him.

Arriving at the private club the McCarthy's belonged to, David found himself ushered into a small private room, where McCarthy was waiting. Scotch firmly in hand, and looking like it wasn't his first, Joseph McCarthy, scion of business, fixed him with an intense look.

David, privately hoped, the father wasn't as seemingly off the wall as the daughter. He hadn't seen Karen since the second date disaster, and didn't intend to. Messages from her went unanswered. "I hope that look isn't about me ignoring his daughter," David thought. "I don't want to have that conversation, either."

The small room was cozy, outfitted with leather club chairs, and a fireplace. Not a useful fixture, the fireplace, in South Florida, David noted. McCarthy offered him a drink. David politely declined. "How early do you start? It was 9:00 AM!" he thought.

McCarthy gestured to a set of club chairs, indicating David should sit, and took one for himself. David noticed the man getting paler by the minute. He finished the drink in hand, and set it on a side table.

"David, I want to talk to you about something I have been keeping to myself, for quite a number of years, now." McCarthy began.

David was quiet, giving McCarthy his full attention, but not contributing to the dialogue.

"I knew your parents back when," he began. "We socialized, played golf, and lived near each other, up on the north end." McCarthy meant the north end of Palm Beach Island. He paused, and took a long breath.

"David, I know about your father, beating you," McCarthy said.

David remained silent, digesting this. He knew his father's friends couldn't be ignorant of the beatings. He had heard his father talking to them about it. So what was the purpose of this sudden confession?

The man suddenly seemed to change topic. David wondered if it was the amber fluid in his glass, or jumbled emotions and thoughts he was working through.

"I have cameras in my house," McCarthy said, "hooked up in every room so that nothing goes unnoticed. I am a very wealthy man, and my family's safety is paramount. I have security guards watching everything, 24-7."

"Does your daughter know you keep tabs on her like that?" David said, Now the conversation was taking an unusual twist.

"God, no," McCarthy almost shouted in an explosion of air. "I saw what Karen, and that crazy friend of hers, did the night you came to the house. My security man, brought it to my attention."

Now it was David's turn to be uncomfortable. He looked away from McCarthy's intense gaze, the memory causing a slight shiver to run through him.

"I am sorry about what happened, under my own roof. She is not a bad girl," he said. "She was just misled, by these young hooligans, that seem to be growing in number these days. But that's no excuse."

David raised his eyebrows at the 'hooligans' reference. Interesting comparison. Then he returned his gaze to McCarthy's frowning face, sensing the revelations were not over.

The topic, now wandered back, to David's father beating him. "Emotional jumble," David thought. Hard to form a clear thought, and harder to stay on topic.

"I know what happened to you, the summer before your parents died," McCarthy said. "Your parents next door neighbor, was a government big wig. He had security cameras back then. They were not as common as they are today."

David didn't move, his gaze didn't waiver. It really couldn't, right now. McCarthy's words, had all but frozen him in place. He had seen the cameras back then, and hoped that the final struggle, that occurred the summer he turned 9 years old, was not able to be viewed by them.

McCarthy went on. "When Larry's security camera footage was reviewed that week, he contacted your father. If the gardener hadn't disappeared by then, your father would probably have killed him."

"No worries," David thought coldly, "I took care of that particular disappearance myself."

His father had beaten him that afternoon. Again. His father was helped out by, one of their gardeners, an illegal immigrant. The man had been in David's fathers debt due to his immigration status. Cash payment and no questions asked, equalled cheap labor.

The man had helped David's father tie his wrists to the back shed gazebo while his father beat him with his belt. This was not the first time. The back gazebo, had been his father's location of choice.

His father would make him take off his clothing and then hit him so hard he left bloody welts. That was where those fine scars on his back, buttocks, and legs, came from that people noticed from time to time.

After the beatings Davids' body and mind would be overwhelmed with pain and a bit of shock.

His father would then ask the gardener to untie David, carry or drag him upstairs to his bedroom, and leave him there. That was the routine.

David was nine years old, then. His mother had been the focus of his father's beatings before he turned seven years old. That's when the focus had turned to him. Two years, of increasing violence.

By age nine, David was tall, powerful and showing the talents of a future elite athlete. He presented a better target than the fragile woman. He also had a mind of his own. He wouldn't cow down, to every whim of his father's.

The gardener hadn't done exactly what David's father had directed him to do that day in the summer when David was nine years old. He had something else in mind.

After his father had walked away, the gardener had intended, an assault of his own. He had a past of such crimes, in his native country. A past, unknown to his current employer. These things fell through the cracks, when you weren't here legally. When you didn't fill out a resume and get a background investigation.

Few illegal immigrants were criminals. In David's case, it only took one.

David's hands were still tied together, just not to the solid steel supports of the gazebo. The man had dragged him a bit further to the side of the shed. This would put them out of direct view from the house, but open enough for the gardener to hear anyone approach.

Dizzy and weak, from the beating his father delivered, David wasn't able to fight back. Much. The problem was, that for the young tiger, it wouldn't take much fighting back, at all.

David would be a formidable opponent to several grown men, even in his temporarily disabled state. His Elemental tiger being, would tip the scales drastically. If it had caught David's transformation, their neighbor's camera footage would have been beyond, interesting. Certainly not what a normal 9 year old boy would be expected to do under the circumstances.

The stress of the attempted attack, triggered David's transformation to begin. He knew what was happening. He had been capable of it, since birth.David pulled away and half stumbled towards the back of the shed. There was a tall privet hedge, between the back of the shed, and the next yard. Next to it, was a wall, adding further coverage between his parents home and the next one.

The gardener, jerked the rope that tied David's hands, knocking him off his feet, trying to stop what he thought was David's attempt at escape. As the man landed on him, trying to pin him down on the ground, David gave a last superhuman effort, to move them both, further, behind the landscape shed.

If you had been close enough, you would have heard a loud snarl, followed by a short, guttural scream. Then silence. Perhaps, you could have heard the gardener bleed out, from his torn open throat. You might have heard, a young man, sobbing softly.

You see, David didn't want to kill anyone. Not a human. Never. Ever. There was a fine line, in controlling his tiger being. Losing control and killing, was, against everything he believed in. Even if the man had hurt him. You don't kill humans. He just wanted to best him, and get away.

The camera, would have seen David, come from behind the shed a little bit later, crying, stumbling in the garden dirt to his knees shoulders shaking, naked. His father always beat him, naked. No bloody clothing as evidence. In case anyone was looking for any, evidence that was.

They wouldn't have seen the gardener. Never again, actually. David wondered now, what they must have thought happened, when they saw the security video. If there was audio, they may have heard the tiger burp before the young man appeared from behind the shed again. The blood, was washed away later that day, by a typical afternoon downpour in south Florida.

David remained still, almost motionless. He wasn't sure where this conversation was going.

"We got together, some of us, and had a coming to Jesus talk with your old man if you know what I mean" McCarthy was talking faster now, blinking rapidly, and trying to sell his case for forgiveness. Finally, David understood.

"I took that old belt, he had been hitting you with, and threw it overboard from my boat. Threatened to do the same, to your old man. The guys backed me. We had some mafioso type guys at the club, back then. They would have done it." McCarthy looked up at him, breathing hard, even though he was just sitting there.

He needed David, to forgive him, David got it. David smiled at the mafioso type guys reference. McCarthy didn't know, that Dr. Ma and David, would have been much more dangerous, than some mafioso guys at the club, would have been.

"It's ok, Joseph," he said using the man's first name, to make it sincere. "I survived, and nothing like that happened, again. My father drank too much."

"We just didn't know what else to do, back then. I always wanted to make it up to you. You have been without a father, for most of your life, David. I would like to be here, if you need me. I know its too late, but I am here anyway." McCarthy sagged a bit in his leather club chair. It seemed after he got all that out he was deflated, tired, older even.

"Lets play golf Joseph, okay?" David stood up, putting his hand out to the older man to help him up.

"David?" Joseph said. "One more thing, I have a favor to ask you."

David looked at him, frowning slightly. What else, after all that? "Of course, what is it?"

"Karen is going to South Africa, in a couple of weeks, that Save the Tiger thing." Joseph McCarthy paused, searching for words, it seemed. "I want to know if you will go with her, watch out for her. I am getting to old to travel like that."

David, realized he was staring, somewhat open mouthed, at the older man. McCarthy said, "I know, it seems awkward for me to ask right now, but I would be very grateful to you, and I don't trust anyone else as much."

McCarthy, waved off David's hand, offered to help him up from the chair. He stood a bit shakily and suddenly put his arm around David's shoulders. "Think about it" he said. David nodded in agreement. "I did **not** see *that* coming," he thought. Who was he kidding? He hadn't seen any of the conversation coming.

The two men walked out of the room towards the golf area without another word. What more needed to be said? It was a beautiful day for a round of golf.

Chapter Sixteen - Dr. Ma Remembers

Memories were all she had of him, now. She hadn't seen him for a thousand years. She thought of him, every day. At least once. The painful tug, no longer took her breath, like when he had first gone, from this plane of existence.

Like she and he had once done together, David and she had done for the last thousand years. Helping a human spirit find peace. Taking out the non human perpetrator. Closure for all involved, really. Except the dark spirits that they destroyed. The ones that caused the mayhem. Those spirits didn't enjoy the outcomes for sure.

Memories of battles won, places that had changed forever, civilizations lost, completely washed over her. This was why she didn't think of him, too often.

Her mobile phone rang, interrupting her thoughts. She tapped the screen of the iPad, hanging from the bottom of the kitchen cabinet, in front of her. Winnie's face appeared. "Good morning Winnie," she said. "You are really getting the hang of Face Time."
Winnie frowned slightly. "Right," she said. She tried to indicate a lesser level of enthusiasm,

but Dr. Ma knew better. Ever since she bought Winnie an iPad and hung it in her kitchen, the woman was calling her grandkids every night.

Winnie's daughter, Pat, had told her so. Pat was less than enthused by Winnie's new found tech knowledge. Her kids, were just as bad, as their grandmother. "Talk to grandma," the littlest one would start nagging, right after dinner.

Dr. Ma lifted a paper towel up to her iPad screen, and wiped the bit of dough that stuck there, when she answered Winnie's call. She was baking muffins, and her hands were covered with ingredients.

"Are you making muffins?" Winnie asked. "Bud wants to reserve some, before David gets to all of them."

"Yes," Dr. Ma laughed. "A new recipe. Sweet potato, pecans, zucchini and maple butter."

"Yes!" Bud said, his face appearing, over Winnie's shoulder. "A dozen please!"

"You don't know if they are any good yet, Bud," Dr. Ma replied.

"Please," Bud scoffed and disappeared from the screen view.

"Ok, Winnie," Dr. Ma smiled at her assistant. "I will make a double batch so Bud can have a dozen. But he has to eat them, even if they aren't great."

"We both know, that anything Bud and I don't eat, we can give to David, and it will disappear. He won't approve of the maple butter, of course."

Dr Ma smiled. David broke his raw vegan eating ways for her muffins, but he didn't like her adding sugars. "I am only using a bit, for flavor," she replied. "Besides, he could use some fattening up."

Winnie broke out in laughter at that one. "He is too thin. I don't know how he does it with all the food he puts away."

"He burns it off. Lots of activity." Dr. Ma thought. Like the case they had just finished.

The Oni demon was gone for good. From the human world. They couldn't stamp it out completely, as much as they would like to. Matter only changes form. Who knows what it would come back as, next time.

"Talk to you later then," Winnie said, practically cutting off the end of her sentence as she ended the call.

Dr. Ma smiled. Other than the grandkids, Winnie kept conversations short, and to the point. She put both trays of muffins in the oven, and cleaned up her prep.

Time for her morning run. She loved to put something aromatic in to bake, before going out. The whole house, smelled of her muffins when she got home. It was comforting. She had lived alone so long. David would stay over now and then, but the two couldn't live together. Too distracting.

She ran south first, down through the neighborhood in West Palm Beach. Then she ran through coastal Lake Worth. Turning east, she was moving fast, up and over the Lake Worth Bridge. One, two, three, four, five strides as she ran, per breath. Fast. Less to think about now that the murder case was closed.

Heading north along A1A she waved and said hello to all the exercisers on this stretch of Palm

Beach Island. Racing up Sloan's Curve and along the water, the glare of the sun on the ocean, hit her. Glittering shards of light, nearly penetrated her dark sunglasses, as they tried to work their way around her ball cap.

A pack of cyclists passed her from behind, as she dipped down to the left, and headed for Southern Boulevard. She was running fast next to the roadway. There was no sidewalk, or extra space, for a runner in the road, during this stretch.

Tam pulled up next to her on his bike. "Ma-sama," he said smiling.

She realized he must have hung back from the pack to speak to her. "Hi Tam, how's the morning ride?" She knew he could catch them easily, after they spoke.

"Any day riding, is a good day," Tam replied.
"So, everything worked out, well?"
"Very," Dr. Ma replied. "Thank you, for arranging assistance from your family." The trees that helped Dr. Ma and David in their investigation, were all, technically, Tam's family.
"Anytime," he said smiling. Tam increased his speed rapidly, and was quickly lost to her view. Nobody riding in the group would think twice,

about his coming and going. Tam was a leg-endary cyclist, known for his blistering speed. If, they only knew why. "Wind child," Ma thought as she turned the corner by Trump's place.

Running west on the Southern Boulevard causeway, she glanced towards the murder scene. Everything was peaceful today. Half a dozen men, were fishing off the bridge. She carefully negotiated the fishing poles, that ille-gally, took up most of the sidewalk. Nothing was ever done about the poles, fish guts, and ever present hazard of being knocked into traf-fic, if you or one of the men mis-stepped.

She headed south on Flagler for the final stretch home. As she neared Jamil's tree, she slowed to a walk. Stopping, she climbed up on the curve of concrete that formed a barrier, the seawall, between the tree and the Intracoastal waterway.
Dr. Ma sat on the wall between Jamil's tree and the waterway. The Elder Sprite, who had spo-ken to David about the shadow killer, bobbed in the water about 10 feet away. Jamil watched Ma silently, patiently waiting if she wanted to talk about the murder case.

The case, was not the first thing, on her mind. Other matters were pushing past, to the surface.

Ma was deep in thought. She remembered him, her love, her mate, whom she had hunted evil demons with, for almost a millennia, before he passed to another realm. He was, now, well beyond her ability to communicate. Too many layers between them, even though she knew he was still there, without her.

Recently she was feeling more attracted to David. She had felt this at different times during the past thousand years. She never acted on it. Neither had David. She knew their eternal balance, or elements, affected him even more than it did her. They lived apart. It was best that way. She just wondered why things seemed different lately. More intense?

She shook off that train of thought, and refocused on her lost mate.

After a successful hunt with David, finding and eliminating an otherworldly bad guy, Ma would try to communicate with her lost love. "We only know, what we know," she thought. "Maybe he can hear me, or sense me. Maybe I can make contact, someday."

The two otherworldly creatures keeping her company, said nothing. They could see she was deep in contemplation. Never disturb a dragon deep in thought. Not your smartest move, ever.

Her mind wandered back to the murder case, and the people involved. Dr. Ma found this whole revolution of human events, fascinating. She and David lived millennia or longer. Humans got a much shorter time on earth. They lived their re-manifestations out in faster time frames.

Humans lived, maybe, 90-100 years at most, depending on what you had to do, while you were here. They came back again and again in reincarnation, trying to get things right. So they could move on to other things. Eventually they ran out of things to do in this realm and moved on to another.

Or, they didn't move on. Ma knew, many that would not accept, that they were free to roam about the Universe. You must be willing to see things, as they were. A journey to learn and progress. Some were stuck in time and stuck in space as well. Human's called them ghosts.

Ma turned her head, towards the bright South Florida sun. Cooler weather today, kept it pleasant in the brilliant blue afternoon, of her day off. She and David took one full day off every week, if possible, to recharge, be alone, restore balance.

The peaceful heaviness of the quiet afternoon wrapped her in its it embrace. She swayed softly with the natural rhythm of the Earth's energy. Jamil waved his branches in harmony with her. Even the Elder Sprite, closed it eyes, and gave in the to soft susurrus of the waves.

Safe in the company, of the two otherworldly entities, she slipped backwards in time.
They walked slowly, up the narrow dusty trail. She was not called Dr. Ma then. Her name was something else, something irrelevant to time, and thus forgotten. He walked beside her, an old man. Bent, and dressed in a dusty robe. Raw silk, a soft off white in color, the robe rustled with his short strides to keep up with her.

She was young then, newly formed and magnificent. A massive wingspan and glittering black scales, set off the lapis blue eyes. They were unchanged, those eyes, even today. She didn't appear very human then. Changes had been wrought through the millennia. She had evolved.

They paused at the end of the path. A rough gash in the mountain, it seemed, where the path cut through the rocky prominence in front of them. The route went no further. It disappeared steps from where they stood. A sheer cliff ran below the drop off.

He looked at her and smiled. It was rare for him. His expression usually carried, the seriousness of his responsibilities.

He touched her shoulder. It was time. Stepping lightly off the path into nothingness, she took flight.

Hours later, still sitting in the same place, on the seawall, Dr. Ma opened her eyes, and stood up in one fluid movement. After so long immobile, she moved again, with speed and grace, as if it had been seconds.

Well, for her, millennia old, it really had been seconds hadn't it? The Sprite Elder slipped slowly beneath the waves with a slight nod in Ma's direction.

Jamil made no change, he was deep in thought, and would probably stay that way for a while. The tree occupant, had different priorities than she did. Endless time and stillness, stretched before it. There was never a rush.

It was time for a sweet potato, pecan, zucchini, and maple butter muffin. One was calling her name from her kitchen counter. Maybe she would invite David over, to try her new recipe. He was always up for her cooking.

Dr. Ma turned, and headed for home. Goodbye for now.

Epilogue

He watched her pass him, and make the southbound turn onto Flagler Drive. She was running
fast. She looked beautiful to him, she always
had. For two thousand years, she had changed
very little.

The fisherman, whose body he had temporarily
borrowed, faced south along the Intracoastal
waterway. The man, was standing, with several
others and their collection of poles, boxes and
buckets of fish guts on the Southern Boulevard
causeway bridge.

The Elemental looked left, towards the recent
crime scene, where she and her current tiger
companion, had recently helped the local police. He wanted to be there, helping her. Helping her, as they had for a thousand years. Before he had been pulled to a realm, where they
could no longer be together.

She had thought he was gone, out of her reach.
Technically this wasn't true. Dragons could
pass between realms. She could abandon her
job here and come to him. Which was why he
never let her know this. As much as he wanted
to be with her, she was needed here.

He could come here and observe her. Borrowing a living host to cohabitate with for an hour or so. He just couldn't re-manifest here. Not with another tiger Elemental here, balancing her Elemental dragon. Not while David lived, and continued a cycle of re-birth, paired with her. His dragon.

He looked at her again, sitting by a large and ancient tree. He recognized the guardian contained there. Jamil. They had worked with Jamil many times. The guardian knew he was here, but did not acknowledge him. For her sake, mostly.

Stepping backwards out of the fisherman, he disappeared from this realm. For now.

The man, rolling some spare fishing line, felt a tug. It was as if he had fallen asleep, leaning on the bridge rail, holding his spare line.
The strange odor of a a large wild animal, came to him on the gentle South Florida breeze. "Did one of those crazies in Palm Beach keep a tiger in their back yard, over there, to his left? Maybe that Trump guy?

The smell, was familiar to him, suddenly. He took his little daughter to the Dreher Park Zoo almost every weekend. She was obsessed with the tiger exhibit. He knew the smell of a big cat well. Looking around and seeing nothing out of the ordinary, and, not getting a whiff of the tiger again, he returned to rolling his spare fishing line.

About the Author

Lenore Maio is a Florida Licensed Acupuncture Physician residing in Palm Beach County Florida, the setting for the Dr. Ma Mystery Series books.

Dr. Maio worked in emergency field medicine and law enforcement before attending graduate school and opening her Traditional Chinese Medical practice. Her speciality is Sports and Functional Medicine.

She lives with her spouse, two dogs and two cats along with an assortment of plants and outdoor critters to keep her company.

Dr. Maio is a long distance runner and cyclist as well as an avid gardener.

See more about the author, and other books she has written, at www.drmamysteries.com.

Coming soon...

"A Point In Time"
Book Two in the Dr. Ma Mystery Series

Preview

Introduction....from Dr. Ma

"How do you get a job like mine? I don't re-member ever applying, or growing up thinking, that is what I was going to do."

"Actually I don't every remember growing up. Because I didn't. Grow up that is. I remember being an Elemental spirit. Created from the el-ement Air."

"I was formed into being for a purpose. My job. By a powerful Adept. What is an Adept exactly? That is a big question for sure. The title Adept applies to those, proficient in some form of what humans would call, magic."

Is changing form, magic? Moving objects? Reading minds? Changing minds? Changing time? Making something like me?

There are doubtless hundreds of names for the individual who created this existence I have. I knew him, but I will call him only, Adept.

He did a good job with me. My mate, who is no longer here in this realm, was an Elemental tiger. The replacement for my mate, is David, another tiger, but 1,000 years younger than me.

My name is Dr. Ma. I am an Elemental, in the form of an Air dragon. David is an Elemental, in the form of an Earth tiger.

We both appear in human guise on the earthly plane of existence.

All three of us turned out pretty damn awesome. In fact, our Adept did a great job. I have accomplished amazing things to help humans in my time. I am not even tired of being here after 2,000 years.

I would like a bit more change. Don't get me wrong. I am talking about the repetition of catching non human killers. That's the job.

There are never the same people, when I come back. Not too bad if you don't become attached to anyone, from the last time. I will miss Winnie, my clinic manager and assistant, and Jeremy, from this life. Jeremy Brenner is a talented young man and fun to work with. He is the cop who helps us with the murder cases. Or, do we help him?

Winnie and I, have become close. As close as something of my nature can become with any human.

David, my constant companion, will be coming with me. I was paired with him a thousand years ago. I miss him briefly, when he re-manifests in a human manner, by being born. Some strange, earth element requirement, birth.

Buddha said something to the effect that the pain humans suffer was primarily from attachment. As a non human, living out a human existence to do my job, I can attest to that.

Don't bother to correct me, on quotes or texts about Buddha, or anyone from the past. I was there. I have always been here it seems. So unless you were there, *hush*. Things change through the millennia in translation. You will most likely be wrong.

I have brilliant friends and acquaintances that cannot remember what was in their last meal, what composed yesterday's activity or be able to access long term information, like special days in their life, correctly. Their mind is crowded with formulas, equations and ideas for world peace.

Try it over a thousand years or more. Wade through that many memories, and thoughts, to remember if it was a bagel or a danish with coffee, you ate for breakfast.

Every day, I am inundated with human surety, that God, Buddha, Yaweh or whomever '*said exactly this or that* and *meant exactly this or that.*' Trust me, those guys barely remembered what *they* had for breakfast. I knew them. I was there. They had more important thoughts crowding their heads.

You will be back when you die. Maybe not as aware as I am. So remember that you pre-plan what you will experience, and learn each time around. I say make a good job of it while you are here each time! Surprise yourself with your success. Or not.

Chapter One - In the Aftermath

Louhu Valley Tiger Reserve, South Africa………

Soft lips swept over her collarbone, leaving chills in their wake. His arms wrapped around her, gently holding her, but with unmistakable power. She felt his hands on her back through the thin cloth of her shirt.

She knew from those hands touching her elsewhere, that they were hard and calloused, but strangely smooth, no roughness to the callouses.

She shivered again, feeling an odd sense of fear mingle with the sexual excitement, that had raised the hairs along her skin, wherever his hands and lips had passed. She opened her eyes as the fear grew more persistent. Gorgeous, tanned skin over rippling back muscle, and tousled blond hair greeted her gaze. His lips travelled down past her collarbone, and continued south along her body.

He was stunning. She had seen him often at events around Palm Beach this past season. Tall and imposing, with deep blue eyes and graceful movements, he was the desire of many of the women, and men she knew. David was his name, an orphan of a wealthy family, he was a generous philanthropist and her Save the Tiger Foundation needed the money he donated.

After, they spent time talking, at one of her events, she found out that he had lived next to her parents, until he was about 9 or 10 years old. But that was all she knew. She had no memory of meeting him in the past. Her father remembered him well, but was strangely reticent when she asked him to share details.

"Karen" she had introduced herself finally bold enough, or desperate enough to get to know him. They had talked, forever it seemed, about her travels through the African continent, helping big game animal conservation efforts. She knew one of his patients, who also travelled to Africa for conservation. David was a local Acupuncture physician. He didn't live off his substantial wealth, like so many kids she grew up with.

She and he had tried a couple botched dates, and she thought that was it. Until, her father had asked David to come with her to South Africa. To protect her, on her trip to a tiger reserve. There had been some recent violence in the area against tourists. As a favor, her father told her about asking David.

She couldn't believe this was finally happening. That was all she had thought of, sexual intimacy with him. Even when he wouldn't talk to her before the trip.

In Africa, so far from home, she was in his arms. His raw power, as he embraced her, reminding her of what she had witnessed. What she thought she had witnessed. "Was it yesterday morning? Had things happened so fast?" Her thought process, was not working right. "Trauma had fried some of her brain wires," she thought.

The calm of their camp shattered by gunfire, screaming, and the smell of blood and fear.

She had stood rooted to the spot, in front of her tent, when she saw David, run in to the center of the melee. He had looked at her briefly, then turned away. Jumping towards the military style truck that had been regurgitating men with guns, she thought she saw him become a very large tiger.
"No, that could not be right!" She was in shock. Nobody can just turn into a tiger. She definitely, did-NOT,-see-that. Piles of bodies had been strewn around the camp, some torn to shreds, guns useless at their sides. "Had she seen that?"

Now, the two of them were back here at the game reserve lodge, in her room. She remembered being carried away from the camp. Fast. "But they had been almost 50 miles northeast from the Reserve!" Someone had been carrying her, and running. "Who? David?"

He pressed against her as he picked her up off the floor, her legs wrapped around his waist. She had dreamed of being with him. "The two of them were about to, what?" Her mind was pulled back, to the gruesome scene at the camp. "How had she gotten here? Were all her men from the camp, here? Or, were they among the dead?"

David kissed her mouth, slowly. Her body turned to liquid in his arms. Warm, and spilling down over him, melting them together. "It didn't matter what had happened, did it? All that mattered, was right now."

For further updates go to
www.drmamysteries,com.

Get on the author's mailing list, read her blog,
learn about new titles coming out!

Thank you for being a fan!